COMIN' DOWN THE ROAD

Queer SF on the Highways and Byways

FRANK SLATER
J. W. STEED

Comin' Down the Road published in 2026
by Peter Schutes Publishing

Slapjack
Copyright © 2026 by Frank Slater

A Globe, Granite Underfoot
Copyright © 2026 by J.W. Steed

All rights reserved.

No part of this publication may be reproduced, distributed, or transmitted in any form or by any means, including photocopying, recording, or other electronic or mechanical methods, without the publisher's prior written permission, except as permitted by U.S. copyright law.

The story, all names, characters, and incidents portrayed in this production are fictitious. No identification with actual persons (living or deceased), places, buildings, and products is intended or should be inferred.

This book is for ADULT AUDIENCES ONLY. It contains substantial sexually explicit scenes with multiple partners and graphic language, which may be considered offensive by some readers.

All sexual activity in this work is consensual, and all sexually active characters are 18 years of age or older.

ISBN: 978-1963667738

CONTENTS

SLAPJACK

BY FRANK SLATER

"Get out of the fucking car!" Alastair stood towering over the open window of the cherry red sedan. His command was returned with silence. He said it again.

"Wait, what? You can't be serious." The man inside the vehicle's voice trembled with fear. His question was alarmed but quiet.

Again, Alastair repeated himself, this time reaching through the open window and lifting the handle to open the door from the inside. The man inside clawed at the automatic window button in a futile attempt to get it up. Alastair's hand was already inside and opening the door.

The man sat frozen and Alastair had to reach over his lap to unfasten the seatbelt.

"Don't just sit there, baby. Get the fuck out!"

A sweat soaked brow nodded but he still didn't move. With deft hands Alastair grabbed him by the upper part of his arms and dragged him to the curb. Cars behind them started honking as the light turned green. The guy on the side of the road was crying in disbelief while Alastair flipped off the growing line of cars, got in the driver's seat, and pulled off into traffic. Only when he was half a block down the road did the owner of the vehicle stand up and start shouting for his car back. It was too late. Alastair was pulling onto the freeway heading east, the one that led out of town.

With the windows still down and the exhaust from the road blowing in, he reached for the radio dial and turned the music way up. Simultaneously he hit the gas and accelerated into the fast lane without bothering to signal. The car had pep. The sound system was good. And the wind in his hair provided sweet relief to the heat of the city, one which he would be leaving behind as the freeway opened up to the suburbs and then to the deserts of the southwest.

He drove for an hour and a half before pulling over to a rest stop. Of course, the car hadn't had a full tank of gas. No matter how smoothly things went, there was always a hitch. He threw a twenty on the counter without comment other than the pump number and withdrew to the car to fill the tank and squeegee the windows. It was still going to be a long ride.

Gassed up, he got back in the car to pull around behind the station. Making sure there was no one else around he pulled a screwdriver from his pack and went to work removing the license plates, replacing them with Arizona plates he had acquired earlier. If the cops ran them he would still be in deep shit, but that would be less likely to happen once he crossed the border in a few hours.

After tossing the old plates in the dumpster he hit the blinker and pulled back onto the onramp, driving cautiously, so as not to draw any unwanted attention. Once back on the highway he abandoned caution and hit the accelerator, barreling to the east as the sun began to go down behind him. The open road was a sweet sensation after so long on the stifling streets of the run-down city. Farms peppered the surrounding landscape as buildings dropped away and the population thinned. After all the drama of the last months, leaving the city behind was a welcome change. There was nothing left for him there. And the excitement of not knowing what awaited him at the next stop was exhilarating. New blood, that's what he needed. And where better to find it than in a city he had never spent time in. To be a stranger, anonymous, and a piece of fresh meat, always turned on those who had been banging away at the same old grind for God knows how long. Just the thought of it made him rise.

He sped up and overtook a semi crawling up the hill in the slow lane. As he approached the border he knew that driving in the fast lane wasn't tolerated the way it was in California, but he still had miles to go before he would have to worry about that. Once in the passing lane he rammed the accelerator down with renewed fervor, and at the same time fondled with his zipper to relieve himself of the growing constraint of his pants.

Freeing his cock from his jeans he yanked at himself as the car moved faster into the growing dusk. With his knee on the steering wheel he used his other free hand to turn up the radio again. He beat off to the rhythm of the music, taking his time, and imagining that the hills on either side of the freeway were giant legs being spread to let him enter. The car accelerated up to nearly a hundred miles an hour and he closed his eyes thinking of all that Billy ass he was leaving behind, all that newbie ass that would be up ahead, and every hot load he would be spurting onto whoever was willing to take it. He shot onto the floor between the brake and the gas as he reached the border and the landscape lit up with the lights of gas stations lining both sides of the road. He rubbed it into the floor mat with his left boot and slowed down slightly, so as to avoid any run in with the highway patrol that was probably lurking in wait behind the overpasses.

Arizona. He had made it. And with the new plates on the car he hoped that he was blending in like any other local. The listed gas prices on the signs was cheaper. The desert behind them was a wide expanse with Saguaro dotting the hills, an open stretch of possibility, so different than the building-filled horizons that he was leaving behind. And whatever was happening in that city back there didn't matter now. He was leaving all of that behind.

Long before hitting the city the urban sprawl began and with it the traffic. Alastair slowed the car to a crawl and the desert heat hit him like a furnace. Glancing around at the other people in the thick line of cars he saw that everyone either had the windows up, and presumably the AC blasting, or their windows were down and they seemed to be used to it. Loosening his collar he thought about how long it would take to acclimate. No doubt there was probably lots he didn't know about this city yet, and he wasn't even properly there.

As he scanned the traffic he spotted a highway patrol car with the officer inside doing the same. He turned his head to avoid eye contact, but for a second he could have sworn that it was a Billy. Maybe it was, and that was a good sign, but for now he could do nothing. The row of cars started moving again, albeit slowly, and Alastair went with the flow. First things first, he would need to ditch the hot car, maybe find himself a new one. And he was getting hungry. Not knowing where he was headed was freeing, but it also came with the inconvenience of not knowing where to go.

The traffic cleared up for a while and then thickened again and started flowing like syrup as the mass started entering the city proper. The area looked industrial and he started making his way to the slow lane to look for an exit. Repeatedly, cars sped up to block him from changing lanes and he had to nudge his way in to the sound of horns. So, driving in this city was much the same, maybe he had just exchanged one backdrop for another. He hoped for more.

Finally, he got all the way over and signaled his intent to exit at the next offramp. At the moment, any direction was as good as another, but he hoped to find a shady looking place to unload the vehicle, or at least somewhere where he could pick up another, less flashy ride.

The streets were long and straight, lined on either side with warehouses and abandoned buildings. He drove parallel to the highway, still heading toward the city, but moving much faster now that he was on the streets. Train tracks crisscrossed some of the intersections and several times he had to wait at a red light to let them pass. It was slow going but he wasn't in a hurry.

Several more lights up and he found what he was looking for. A warehouse with an open door revealed cars up on jacks inside, various vehicles in the parking lot with their hoods up, and a few guys in mechanic's jumpsuits smoking cigarettes under an awning that was barely providing shade. *This is it*, he thought, and pulled into the packed parking lot.

With any luck these guys were running a chop shop. From the sight of the place it sure looked like it, but there was only one way to find out. The men eyed him suspiciously as he pulled in. His ride was much newer than the others in the lot, and from the sound of the engine was clearly running just fine.

Alastair parked halfway through the lot and walked the rest of the way to where the men stood. He didn't bother to lock the car and left the keys in the ignition. As he approached, one of the men threw his cigarette butt into a rusty can and lit another. Alastair did the same, pulling a smoke from his pack and offering the few that were left to the other guys standing around. Two of them shook their heads but a third pulled one from the pack and struck a match to light it.

"You're not from around here are you?" said the man between puffs.

Alastair looked him up and down as the others stood silently.

"How can you tell?"

The guys laughed at his response. "You're all pasty white. Obviously, you're not a desert rat."

Alastair looked down at his arms, realizing that the guy was right. They all had deep tans from years in the desert sun. He looked like he spent most of his waking hours at night.

"Yeah, yeah, you got me. Sure, I'm new around here. But I don't see what difference that makes. Which one of you is the owner of this place? See that car over there..."

The guy who had spoken before cut him off, "Who wants to know?"

"Just point me to the owner, my business is with him."

The guy he was talking to shrugged and the others murmured but none gave him an answer. As he was about to make his way into the garage a taller man, similarly dressed in a mechanic's jumpsuit exited the building into the harsh sunlight.

"Ok guys, smoke break's over. Get back to work." He eyed Alastair suspiciously. "And who are you?"

Alastair gave him the look that said, 'don't fuck with me' and pointed to the red car that stood out like a sore thumb in the lot of partially dismantled cars. "I'm trying to unload my car. Figured that this might be a good place to do some business."

"And what makes you think that? The car hot?" The other men had gone back inside and this guy wasn't looking any friendlier. "What makes you think this is that kind of place?"

Alastair adjusted his tone, "I'm not presuming shit, my friend. But it's a good car and I need to swap it out for something else, something a little less flashy. We could both come up."

The guy wiped sweat from his brow, adding a fresh streak of grease to his forehead. His look was classic mechanic, dirty hands and all, and Alastair flashed a smile thinking about how manly the guy looked all glistening with sweat in the hot sun.

"Ok, why don't you come inside and show me if you have anything to sweeten the deal and tell me a bit about this car you're trying to unload." Without saying anything more he headed toward the door back into the garage, motioning for Alastair to follow.

Alastair didn't hesitate, getting out of the sun was a welcome prospect. The door to the left of the massive garage door led into the office portion on the building. Inside it smelled like tires and stale coffee. The room was mostly empty aside from a percolator bubbling away and a few posters which either had cars zipping down empty highways or touristy postcard photos of the surrounding mountains.

The mechanic went to the connecting door and shouted for one of the men to inspect the sedan outside then came back and gestured for Alastair to sit across the desk before sitting down himself.

"You're obviously not from around here. What made you decide to come to my shop?" The question was an accusation.

Alastair looked him dead in the eyes. "Look, man, your shop just happened to be the first one I came across when I got to the city. Yeah, the car's hot. It's from Cali. So am I. I'm not looking for some huge score, I just need to swap it out for something less conspicuous. Planning on being in town for a while, I need wheels. But that flashy beast out there won't do. Trying to keep a low profile. I'll let it go for cheap. Or for something to get me around that isn't so hot."

Wheels began to turn in the man's head. He got up and poured himself some coffee into a little Styrofoam cup without offering any to Alastair.

"And you just assume that that's what I do here, huh? Any other assumptions I should know about?" Now he was leaning on the edge of the desk looking down at Alastair. The silence filled with the hum of an unseen air conditioner.

Alastair let the question hang in the air between them for a moment. "I'm not the type to assume shit. Help me unload this vehicle and I can help you out in other ways."

The mechanic went back to the door to the garage and leaned in, "Give us a few in here. And get those brake pads on, the client is coming back for that one soon." He shut the door behind him then went to the front and locked the latch before pulling the blinds down a little further.

"Other ways, huh?"

When he turned around Alastair was already on his knees and pulling at the long zipper that led down the front of the blue jumpsuit. The mechanic freed the suit from his shoulders and let it drop from there. He reached a greasy hand up to the back of Alastair's head and guided him to his stiffening cock.

Alastair took him into his mouth and felt the hard throb of the man quickening. By the time it hit the back of his throat it was fully hard, beading pre-cum onto his tongue. He dove in further and felt the head pass his tongue into his throat, leaving it there for a moment and swallowing to tighten around the mechanic's dick, then pulling back slowly and doing it all over again.

The mechanic moaned in pleasure and gripped Alastair's hair, pushing him back in for more. When he was about to burst he pushed again, this time harder, and held him there, mouth up against his crotch while he pumped hot streams, one after another, into Alastair's open throat. Alastair swallowed without choice or hesitation, lapping up every last drop.

Without a word the mechanic went back to the window and pulled the blinds back up, gazing into the parking lot at Alastair's ride, which one of the men had pulled up to the garage door and was beginning to inspect.

He took another sip of his coffee and said, "Yeah, I'm sure we can work something out. Did you want a new ride or cash? Either way it won't be much. Think of it as a fee for the extra hoops I'll have to jump through to unload the car." He waited expectantly without bothering to look back at Alastair.

Alastair needed a vehicle and cash. But obviously he wouldn't be getting both here. "I'll take a car, what do you have?"

"Let's go out back and I'll show you what I've got. Like I said, it won't be much." He led Alastair through the garage, which was filled with the sounds of men working. At a gesture of the hand one of the mechanics pulled the red sedan into the garage and set to work stripping it, wasting no time.

They exited through another door in the back which led into another small lot surrounded with chain-link fence topped with barbed wire. Nearly a dozen cars sat there rotting in the sun. None of them looked great, but they did all have the advantage of not sticking out with any bling.

"Take your pick. I can gas'um up for you but that's the best I can do for ya. None of these are hot as far as I know, so there's that." He pulled a cigarette from one of the jumpsuit's many pockets and started puffing on it while Alastair walked through the lot to make his selection.

A soccer mom looking hatchback caught his eye. No cops would think to tail a station wagon. It wasn't exactly sexy, but it had four wheels and it would give him time to check out the city without worrying about getting pinched. He wouldn't need it for long anyway, not once he got to know the lay of the land and all the right spots.

"I guess this one'll do."

The mechanic went back inside for a moment without saying anything. When he returned he pitched the keys at Alastair who caught them midair. He went to the gate and swung it open to let Alastair down the alley back to the road.

"We're done here. And that's the last I want to see of you around here. Don't think about coming back. I run an honest business and don't need your kind fucking that up."

Alastair got behind the wheel and turned the key.

❋   3   ❋

The station wagon felt like driving a tank after zipping through the freeways in the last car. It had no pep. The AC didn't work. And even worse, some of the windows wouldn't go down. But it didn't stick out in any way, and that's what he needed, at least for now. He pulled back onto the long six lane drag that led into the city. The sprawl was insane, and it seemed like he drove for hours before the buildings sprouted up from the landscape, finally adding a little bit of shade to the relentless sunny streets.

The light turned red and he slowed down, the brakes screeching to be replaced with a piercing whine. The guy at the mechanic's had sure come up, even if unloading the car was going to prove difficult. But the station wagon was legal; he even had a pink slip. It would allow him a moment to settle in and get the lay of the land without having to worry about the fuzz. And just as he was thinking this, he looked into the rearview mirror and saw a highway patrol cruiser behind him. The light turned green and he hit the gas gently, not wanting to draw any undue attention.

Traffic was still thick even though rush hour was just getting started. At least he wouldn't have to worry about speeding. But block after block the cruiser stayed on his tail. Alastair wasn't quite sure where he was headed, but he had to scope out different parts of the city, find all the right places, find a place for himself. Most of the neighborhoods he had seen so far looked much the same, industrial and run down. And it was damn hot. The more he drove the more he thought about how good a cold beer would feel running down his throat.

Getting sick of the cop riding his ass he decided to take a left down a residential street, hoping to shake him. Even through the street led him away from the highway the cruiser took the left with him, running the yellow to stay on him. Alastair's sweat ran into his eyes, causing them to blur for a moment.

Bhheeew.

The patrol cruiser's lights went on. Alastair blinked to see if it was real, or if the heat was just getting to him. The siren confirmed his dismay.

"Fuck!"

At least the car was legal, or at least he thought so. And his license was up to date, although out of state. He pulled to the side of the road under the welcome shade of a tree, and waited for that ever so familiar, 'license and registration'. The saying please part was only in the movies.

The highway patrolman got out of his SUV and cop-walked up to the station wagon. But instead of going up to the driver's side window he circled the car looking it up and down suspiciously. While the officer was looking around Alastair remembered that the window wouldn't roll down. It was only going to cause further problems.

The officer knocked on the window, drawing Alastair back to reality, and made a 'roll down the window' motion with his hand.

Alastair spoke loudly, so as to be heard through the glass, "The window is busted. How would you like me to proceed?" He recognized the face on the other side of the glass and had to hold in any sign of recognition and excitement. His earlier suspicions were confirmed. There were Billys on the force.

"Get out of the vehicle." The Highway Patrolman's hand lingered near his gun.

Alastair slowly opened the door and got out. He made sure not to make any quick movements, seeing that the cop was already on edge.

"Up against the car, hands on the roof."

He complied, heart starting to race. The cop used his boot to spread Alastair's legs apart, spreading them a little wider than was comfortable. Alastair's cock stirred. For a moment Alastair thought he might fuck him right there in the middle of the suburban house-lined street.

The officer began a pat down, making sure not to miss any places, even running his hand over Alastair's crotch. His hand lingered for moment on his ass before re-moving his wallet and taking a step back.

"Stay where you are. Don't move."

After scowling at the California identification he re-treated to his cruiser to run the license. The seconds ticked by like hours, and if it wasn't for the shade Alas-tair might have melted where he stood.

After a while the officer came back and tossed the wallet onto the hood of the car.

"I'm going to have to conduct a search. Put your hands behind your back, so I can cuff you while I search the vehicle."

Alastair knew the drill all too well. "What's the problem, officer? I haven't done anything."

"We'll see about that. Your registration is expired, and the last tags were in someone else's name."

"I just bought this car. Seriously, less than an hour ago. I've got the papers and everything." His voice was betraying fear. He had just got here, it was too soon for this shit. And the Billy sure wasn't as welcoming as the ones back home.

The cuffs clicked onto his wrists. "Sit down on the curb and keep quiet while I search the car." Alastair did as he was told and could only hope that there was nothing contraband inside. He hadn't even thought to look before driving off the lot.

The officer opened the backdoor and got inside, rifling through the cracks in the seat and shining a flashlight beneath them. He grunted as he did so, making noises that indicated something, but Alastair couldn't tell what. Getting arrested wouldn't be a good start to finding his way in a new city.

When the officer got out of the backseat empty-handed Alastair breathed a sign of relief. He moved on to the back and opened the hatchback, lifting the lid off of the spare tire wheel well.

Alastair dared to speak up, "Hey officer, aren't you a Billy?"

The officer looked taken aback. He stiffened up, straightening his back, and glared down at Alastair on the curb.

"I'm part of the Cops of the Future program, if that's what you mean. But I told you to shut up. No more out of you until I'm finished here." The cop went back to digging through the trunk. His latex gloves stuck to his hands with sweat.

So, the Billys had been deployed here. Despite every-thing that had happened in California the program was still going strong in other parts of the country. Maybe Arizona had figured that introducing them into the Highway Patrol was less problematic? Or maybe they were being tested in different roles, to see where they could be most effective. Having proved wildly unpop-ular in California, despite the apparent drop in crime rates, Alastair was curious if the scandal had spread to other cities. The Billy obviously didn't want to talk about it.

He finished with the search, coming up with nothing and clearly annoyed to have nothing to base an ar-rest on.

"You've got two weeks to get your registration in order. And you're going to need an Arizona license if you plan on staying for an extended length of time." He removed the cuffs from Alastair and allowed him to stand. His legs were cramped from sitting for so long on the scolding concrete. "And I don't want to see you again around here. You're obviously not from this neighbor-hood and I'm sure they don't want you lurking around either. Scram."

Alastair looked at him with that *look*, implying that their business wasn't finished. He stood still waiting for the Billy's next move.

"What? You think we're not done here?"

Alastair looked down at his feet, running his eyes down the front of the uniform, pausing for an ever so brief moment on the cop's crotch. He knew exactly what he was packing underneath, and it had been too long since he had had a taste. He spoke to the ground, "I was thinking that..."

"We're done here. Get lost. And consider yourself lucky that you're getting off with a warning." The officer turned around and went back to his cruiser. He got behind the wheel and fiddled with his radio, but didn't turn the vehicle back on. He was clearly going to wait for Alastair to leave.

❧ 4 ❧

Alastair pulled back onto the main drag and the Billy tailed him for a few blocks, just to make him sweat, before the cruiser finally veered off to head in the opposite direction. The expired tags were going to be a problem, they might attract a Billy's attention, but it wasn't a good way of casting the line. Clearly the Billys here weren't so easy a target. Perhaps they had been apprised of the scandal and had been ordered to keep their pants on, so to speak.

It was well over a hundred degrees outside, and it was way hotter in the station wagon.

"This piece of crap. I'm gonna need a better ride." Alastair spoke to himself, competing with the volume of the radio. And his next stop damn well wasn't going to be the DMV. He didn't just need a better car, he needed something to drink. A cold beer would hit the spot, and so would some welcome shade. The Billy had left him hot and bothered, and obviously hot had a whole other meaning here.

Making sure to drive at exactly the speed limit he drove in the middle lane, unsure where he was going and wanting to make sure that he didn't miss a turn if he found a place that looked inviting enough. After such a long drive he needed to piss. And he was hungry. Every

20

function of his body cried out for relief. Perhaps he could find a place to satiate every need.

After a few miles he saw a bar with darkened windows with a sign that announced happy hour beers and free pool for customers. He pulled up to the curb out front and dropped a few quarters in the meter. Nothing like having to pay to get out of your car. And his money was running low. He'd have to be convincing at the bar, or find someone to roll over once it got dark.

He strolled in to the welcome blast of AC and the low light of a proper drinking establishment. There were only a few guys standing around the pool table but the music was loud. The barkeep stood near the end of the bar, polishing a glass and hardly looking up as the spear of light from the door stabbed into the darkness.

Alastair moved down toward the tender and took a stool in front of him. The man still didn't look up and had obviously perfected that bartender skill of looking busy while avoiding pouring a drink even though no one else was waiting.

Alastair spoke over the music, "How about a beer? I sure could use a cool down."

The barkeep didn't say anything but moved over to the taps and started to fill a pint. He brought it over to Alastair and asked, "You want to start a tab, or are you paying cash?"

Alastair threw a ten on the bar. The bubbly head of the beer spilled over the brim and started to pour down the side of the glass. Alastair slid it over to him and slurped at the head until his mouth was full of cool froth. He lifted the glass and took a long draught. The cold beer ran down his throat and he could feel its effect all through his body. There was nothing like a cold beer on a hot day. He downed the rest of the pint in a few swigs and tapped on the empty pint glass to get the bartender's attention. Pointing to the glass he mouthed the word, "another."

Picking up the second pint he moved over to the pool table where the men stood around smoking without speaking. One of them moved a pool stick back and forth and sank the six ball in one smooth stroke. He sunk three more balls before finally missing and handing the stick to the next guy.

"Nice shot." said Alastair.

The man smiled at him but didn't reply. The way he moved around the table suggested that he was a regular and could probably navigate the bar with his eyes closed. Alastair liked the way he looked. Muscular arms, straight posture. A man with confidence in his own movements. The kind of guy that was good in bed and didn't carry any shame or self-consciousness with him.

Even though Alastair only had a few bucks left he offered to buy the guy a beer.

"I'll take whiskey, if you're buying." His voice was deep.

Alastair didn't hesitate, and for good measure bought himself a third beer. When he returned with the drinks the man was taking another shot, but missed the pocket and moved back over to Alastair.

"How about a smoke on the back porch." It wasn't a question.

Alastair followed him through the empty bar to the back door. As it opened light cut through the darkness, for a moment letting in a harsh reminder that it was still afternoon outside. The heat followed in a startling blast.

"Don't worry, there's umbrellas out here." He motioned to a picnic bench that was fortunately bathed in shade.

Both of them sat down, drinks sweating in their hands. Alastair pulled out his pack of smokes, took one for himself, and offered one to his companion.

"Name's Alastair. Want a smoke?"

While he lit his, the man took one and did the same. "Ben. My friends all call me Slapjack. Nice to meet ya. I take it you're new around here."

Did everyone have to call him out for not being a local? "Yeah, you got me. Nice to meet you, Slapjack. I knew a Jack once..." He didn't know why he said it out loud, but he couldn't help but think about Jacky. Poor Jacky. He snapped out of it. It was no time for sentimentality. "You come here often?"

"Me and some of the guys are here pretty often, we like to think of this as our place. What brings you here? It's not exactly a tourist friendly spot." He took a long drag of his cigarette.

"Me... well, I just moved here. Just happened to see it when I was ready for a drink. No reason, really."

Ben was looking at him like he didn't believe a word. He took a pull on the whiskey, swallowed, and then downed the rest of the snifter. He swirled the remaining ice around in the bottom of the glass.

"Are you looking for a reason?" The look in his eyes said everything that needed to be said.

Alastair took the bait. "Is there a private place around here?"

"Right here is as private as any. The bar won't mind. Like I said, this is our place."

That was all Alastair needed. He stood up and Ben followed his lead. He finished his beer in one gulp and set the glass down on the table. Ben was already in the corner, face against the wall, and dropping his pants around his knees. Alastair took the cue.

He lowered his own pants, cock already stiffening before it was free. Even though his mouth was dry he managed to collect a bit of spittle, spit it into the cup of his hand and worked it all over the head of his dick. Ben did the same and slathered his puckering asshole. Ben put his hands, open palms, onto the fence as Alastair drew himself nearer and worked the head of his cock into Ben's ass. He was tight and it took a second to find his way in.

"Push." Ben obeyed and he opened up to let Alastair fully inside. Once his cock was in to the hilt he held himself there, feeling himself swell, growing to his full potential. Ben grunted as Alastair started pumping, slowly at first, and then really getting into him. His left hand went to Ben's shoulder, holding him in place and at the same time bracing himself as his legs started to get wobbly. With his right hand he reached around and took Ben's cock into his palm. It had too much girth to fully wrap his fingers around it.

As the size of Ben's dick registered he couldn't hold in any longer and blew his load straight into Ben's still tight ass. He wished that he could somehow keep it up, stay inside, and keep going. But his wet dick slid out and only remained semi-erect.

Without a word he switched places with Ben and lowered his pants a little further. He arched his back in invitation. Ben didn't waste any words and worked his way into Alastair, using the pre-cum that had been worked up to aid his entry.

Alastair could hardly believe that all that dick could fit inside of him. It felt like all of him was filled with cock. So much that he could barely breathe for a second. They were now in full sunlight, that ball of flame having now moved enough to avoid the umbrella completely.

Their sweat intermingled as Ben brought himself in closer and put his arms around Alastair's neck, hanging on as if he might collapse.

As he spurt inside he used Alastair's body to keep him from collapsing at the knees. He shuddered as he came, body harshly jerking with each stream of jizz that shot out of him.

"Now that introductions are through, how about another drink?" said Ben as if nothing had happened.

$\maltese$ 5 $\maltese$

Each of them ordered another beer. Between sips Alastair listened to Ben talk about life in the city, where he had come from, and how he had gotten here. He wasn't the only one to arrive in a hot car, and from what he said the place was worth hanging around, at least for a while.

"And what's the story on the Billys here? I was pulled over, but it didn't go as well as I'd hoped." Alastair sucked down the last of the beer and tapped on the counter for another.

"You mean those Cops of the Future guys that they got working Highway Patrol?"

"Yeah, back home... well, they're a fun ride. They liked to play cat and mouse. But I think their program was canceled. I was surprised to see them have a different role here." His beer arrived and he pointed out that Ben should get one too.

Ben finished his drink. "I know what you're on about. It was all over the TV a few months back. It was around the time they introduced those guys here, what did you call them, Billys? Cloned supercops, or something like that? We heard rumors. But yeah, Highway Patrol, that's the only beat I've seen'um on." A fresh beer arrived and he slurped at the overflowing head. "Hey, you wanna get out of here?"

"I've got wheels but nowhere to go." Alastair did need to find a place to crash.

"Fine. We can grab a bottle on the way to my pad. You got any money?"

Alastair got up and fished the keys out of his pocket. "Not really. You know a way to get some?"

Ben followed suit. "Maybe."

They strode out of the bar and Alastair was surprised that there was still daylight. Around the corner he found his car waiting, complete with fresh parking ticket crimped behind the wiper blade.

"Shit! Those fuckers got me. Damn it!"

Ben laughed. "For real. Is this your ride? What a piece of shit."

Alastair explained the chain of events that had necessitated the beater station wagon. Ben seemed unimpressed by any of it. He kicked the tire of the car, pulled the ticket off of the windshield, tore it up and released it to the wind. The pieces blew down the street toward the setting sun.

"I get it man, but wouldn't you rather ride in style. We can do better than that. And it's still not in your name, right?"

Alastair confirmed Ben's suspicion.

"Ok, let's go find something nicer. Something with some speed." Ben moved on from the car and started walking down the block. Leaning over his shoulder he said, "Aren't you comin'?"

For a minute Alastair hesitated. After all he'd gone through to get the ride it felt weird leaving it behind so soon. Ben just kept on walking. Alastair tossed the keys through the open driver's side window onto the seat. If he was going to abandon the vehicle there was no reason that the next guy couldn't come up.

"Hey wait up." He trotted down the street to catch up with Ben.

The two walked in pace through the dying sunlight. From block to block the neighborhood grew visibly nicer. It looked like a recent wave of gentrification had brought with it the usual boutiques, coffee bars, and furniture shops. It was the same old story from town to town. Benches had been removed to discourage loitering. Patrol cars lazily rolled by, giving the illusion that crime had also been thwarted. The people on the street all looked down, passing each other without comment or eye contact. The cars were also growing visibly nicer as they moved west.

Several times Ben paused to scope out a car, checking for open windows and if any of them had been left running while the owner ran into a shop for a quick errand. Alastair stared at him, his quick movements full of confidence and his little apple ass perfectly contoured by tight pants. It looked like Ben had done this all before. The way he moved didn't even call attention for those passing by.

It was a few more blocks before he halted and said, "This is the one. Puts that beater of yours to shame. This is a ride." It was a sports car with a pull up top. It shined silver in the last of the daylight.

"But the windows are up." Alastair checked the door handle. "And it's locked."

"You new to this or something? Thought you were experienced." Ben pulled a screwdriver from his pocket and slid it in between the window and the lip of the door. With one levered pull, the passenger window cracked silently. He used his elbow to finish the job and pushed the remaining glass inward onto the seat. Reaching inside and opening the door he brushed the shards off the seat and onto the floormat. He deftly picked it up and dumped most of the glass into the gutter by the tire before moving around to the driver's side and motioning for Alastair to get in.

Ben made quick work of the ignition and fired up the engine.

"You'll have to show me that trick. Usually I just drag the driver out of the car and take it from there."

Ben said nothing in return but flashed Alastair a smile. He depressed the accelerator and pulled deftly into traffic, not bothering to use the blinker. "My place then?" Without waiting for an answer he hit the gas and swerved through the line of cars. The speed limit was forty, but he wanted to see what the car could do and brought it up to seventy.

❦ 6 ❦

They weaved through the city streets cutting from lane to lane and instigating a barrage of horns from other vehicles. The evening traffic had thinned out but there were still too many cars to really open it up.

"Let's see what this thing can do." Ben shouted over the hot wind rushing in the windows. Without looking for an answer he veered off toward the freeway. He ran a red right before the onramp and swerved to avoid a pedestrian. Once on the freeway the horizon lit up in the brilliant pastels of sundown. The city below seemed to already be asleep as the car came alive and Ben pushed it further. He sped from the slow lane all the way across the other lanes to the left. Once in the fast lane he really kicked it into gear and Alastair looked over at the speedometer to find that Ben had already crossed a hundred. The car hummed with life. The engine was designed to take it. The pavement rushed below them. Ben pushed his foot down even harder and the needle kept rising. He drove the way he fucked.

They rushed up toward a car that was barely doing sixty-five in the fast lane and Ben gracefully swerved around them, cutting in front once he had passed. The car behind them flashed their lights in warning but neither of them were paying any attention to the stretch of road they were leaving behind.

Alastair leaned over and pulled down the zipper on Ben's pants, using both hands to free his member and unclasping the button so that the zipper wouldn't rub him raw. Once his dick was free he bent down over the center console and took Ben into his mouth. The farther he slid Ben's cock down his throat the faster Ben drove. Egging him on he took one of Ben's hands off of the steering wheel and placed it on the back of his head, used it to push himself farther down, giving Ben his cue.

Ben took the hint and weaving his fingers through Alastair's hair and finding the rhythm that pleased him most. All the while he drove faster and faster, pushing the car to its limits. 110. 115. 120. He closed his eyes and tilted his head back forgetting all about the road as his balls tightened. He wanted it to last and fought to keep from cuming so soon. Alastair dove in further, sucking him down to the hilt.

Bhheeew.

On the other side of the freeway Ben saw a Highway Patrol cruiser flip on his siren and speed toward the next crossing of the divider to cut across and flip a bitch. He pushed the car up to 125 and continued to accelerate as Alastair came up for air wondering what was going on.

"Oh shit, they're on us." Alastair wiped spit from his lips with his sleeve.

Ben kept his eyes on the road. "I've got this. That SUV doesn't have shit on what this ride can do." His cock was still throbbing. It pulsed to the rhythm of his quickening heartbeat.

Alastair reached over and took the spit glistening dick into his hand and started stroking. He was a righty, but did his best to keep a steady rhythm as though he was a born southpaw. He slowly tugged the foreskin all the way down and then back up again, deliberately taking his time to tease Ben and make it last. The slower he went the faster Ben drove. If they hadn't been moving at lethal speed he would have sat up and tried to lower himself onto Ben's lap. He looked around the cab of the car to see if he couldn't pull it off anyway. But the sports car was a bit too small for such maneuvers.

The patrol cruiser had made its way across the divider and was now speeding toward them, weaving through traffic with its light and siren blasting. Alastair wanted to put Ben back in his mouth but wanted to see the action on the road, so kept working with his hand. The patrol cruiser started to gain on them, pushing the vehicle to its limit and racing around any cars that stood between them. Ben worked the accelerator and got the car up to 140 before it started to whine in protest.

"Think you can outrun him?" Alastair shouted over the sound of the engine.

Ben said nothing and focused on the road. His cock stood stiff and pre-cum milked its way out onto Alastair's hand, causing him to speed up his stroke. Ben grunted in anticipation before he finally spoke. "I think so, but there's an offramp coming up that will throw us onto the dirt roads. These guys don't have jurisdiction there. I think I can lose him if we go down the wash." He words came out between heavy breaths. Alastair moved him in steady up and down motions.

The cruiser, stretched to its limits, moved to within a few cars distance from them. Cars caught in the friction of the chase honked in fright, the sound dopplered in long descending streaks.

"There it is up there." The exit was rapidly approaching and Ben swerved into the slow lane, dodging cars as he went.

The patrol cruiser gained one last bit of speed and rolled up right behind them as Ben took the exit. In the rearview mirror Alastair could see the distinct face of a Billy behind the wheel. He wore a look of determination and concentration. Just the sight of him was enough to make Alastair even hotter and he leaned down again to finish Ben off in his mouth. Whatever was happening outside of the car at that moment didn't matter. He wanted to taste Ben at the moment of his climax.

Hot jizz flowed into him in one eruptive spurt. Ben's cock quivered as his balls rose and fell, cupped in Alastair's hand as he worked the last of the cum out of him and swallowed deeply.

❧ 7 ❧

When Alastair came up for air they were off of the highway and speeding down a dirt road. The car rattled horribly as it trundled over the washboarded road, but Ben was trying to pick up speed. The condition of the road was horrible and it would give the cruiser an advantage. Behind them the lights still flashed and they could hear the officer yelling something through the bullhorn. His words were unclear, but it was obvious enough that he was shouting for them to pull over.

"Not on my life, buddy!" Ben spoke to himself as he pushed the vehicle to its limits.

Alastair's heart was racing. "Where are we going?" He shouted over the noise of the car bumping up and down.

"There's nothing out here but dirt roads crisscrossing the desert. I'm just trying to lose this tail." Ben kept his eyes on the road.

The car leapt forward as a loud bang sounded. The road was growing increasingly littered with rocks. The headlights only lit up a few yards in front of them and it was impossible for Alastair to know where they were headed. Hopefully Ben knew where he was going. The cruiser couldn't have been more than thirty feet behind them and was gaining.

Ben veered off to the right, away from the highway. The headlights lit up a patch of desert revealing a wide-open wash extending out before them.

Ben shouted over the noise, "We can lose him down this way."

The cruiser took the turn as well, showering the side of the road with a spray of sand as it skidded around the corner into the wash. To the sides the desert glowed red and blue as the lights of the siren moved in a circular pattern around the scrub. The sand rifts and creosote looked eerie in the light but none of them had time to look. There was a loud clunk as the car hit a rock and the tires began to spin out in a deep patch of sand. It brought them to a standstill and Ben pushed the gas harder, causing the wheels to spin and dig them deeper into the sand. They were stuck.

"Oh shit, what do we do now..." Alastair was already unlocking the door, preparing himself to run. Getting lost by running out into the desert was probably a death sentence, but the Highway Patrol SUV was on them, pulling up right behind the car, unaffected by the deep sand. Four-wheel drive might not mean shit on the highway, but here he had the full advantage.

The spotlight stabbed through the night and lit up the interior of the car. They wouldn't be going anywhere. The officer slowly got out of the cruiser, flashlight and gun drawn. "Get out of the car, slowly. Hands up. Close the doors behind you and then put your hands on the roof of the vehicle." Full cop tone, his deep bass of a voice commanded full attention, but it betrayed a touch of fear. He was outnumbered and in the middle of nowhere, but he advanced on them, gun drawn, as if he had done this a million times.

Alastair and Ben did as they were told. The car was dug in and wouldn't be going anywhere without a tow truck. The cruiser's engine was still running, it was the only sound in the night other than their heavy breathing. The officer approached slowly, weapon still drawn.

"Are either of you armed?" As he spoke he shined the flashlight into their eyes, momentarily blinding them to his face. But Alastair didn't need to see his face to know what he looked like.

They both shook their heads. Receiving the answer he was hoping for the Billy got closer, first frisking Ben and then moving over to the other side of the car to confirm that Alastair wasn't packing heat.

As he patted Alastair down, he couldn't resist goading the Billy. "It's been a while. You don't have to stop there."

The Billy took a step back, uncertain what to do with the comment. Alastair looked over his shoulder at the officer, eyes all doughy with want.

"Shut up. You're under arrest." The officer fiddled with his cuffs, trying to navigate the flashlight and gun at the same time. As usual, officers were used to having backup and wore a specific fear when alone.

Alastair held out his wrists, almost an invitation. "Go ahead. I know you like it that way."

For a moment the Billy looked confused and then a sparkle of recognition registered in his smirk, even though he was doing his best to keep it contained. He clicked the cuffs on and dragged Alastair over to the front of the car. He pushed his head down on the hood, bending him over nearly halfway.

"You stay there. Don't move." He kept his eyes on Alastair as he moved over to Ben and repeated the process.

Once he had his hands secured behind his back he shoved him into the same position as Alastair.

He removed both of their wallets and told them not to move before moving back to the patrol cruiser to run their info. After calling it in he went back to where they remained bent over the hood.

Alastair spoke up again, "I said you can go ahead. I'll bet Slapjack wouldn't mind either." He looked over at Ben who smirked back at him. He took it that the Billy's were also Ben's kind of guys.

Without saying a word the Billy yanked Alastair's pants down around his ankles. For a moment he stared at his pale ass and freed himself from his zipper. His heavy belt clanked in the silent night. Before advancing on him he moved over to Ben and repeated the motion. Both looked so good he froze for a minute, unsure where to begin.

With Ben right in front of him he started there. Ben spread his legs slightly farther to adjust his height, so that the Billy could more easily enter him. The Billy removed a small bottle of lube hidden in his utility belt and squirted a generous amount on his throbbing cock, then adding some to Ben's waiting ass. As he slid inside of him he reached over and applied some of the lube to Alastair's waiting rear as well. So, the Arizona Billys were no prudes either. Their reputation had yet to spread, but they must have been busy all over the city.

Alastair looked over at Ben's face, now contorted with pleasure as it rubbed back and forth on the hood of the car while the Billy moved inside of him to the same motion. He hoped that the officer wouldn't run out of steam before it was his turn. The cuffs were chafing his wrists, so he tried not to move too much, but the anticipation was getting to him. Not only for the fucking he was about to have dished out, but for whatever was going to come after that. The car wouldn't be going anywhere, and they had been caught red handed. Reckless endangerment and grand theft auto. Neither of which were on the Billy's mind at the moment.

The Billy made a 'mmmmh' sound as he pulled out of Ben, obviously having a difficult time holding it but not wanting to waste the opportunity of getting inside of both of them. Alastair looked over his shoulder, back at the officer, and gave him the inciting eye.

"You gonna do this or not?" Before he finished the sentence the Billy was inside of him. The way he fucked was familiar, it had been too long. Ben remained in the same position, panting. The look in his eyes was one of deep arousal, and slight jealousy of only getting to watch now. But Alastair could tell that he delighted in watching and kept his face turned toward him to let him share in the moment.

The officer pounded away for a while, then returned to Ben and started all over again. After several minutes of slamming his cock into Ben's wanting ass he moved back to Alastair, and repeated the process until he couldn't take it any longer and pulled out, shooting his load all over the hood of the car between their prone faces.

He stepped back to catch his breath as he yanked up his zipper and repositioned his belt. The Billy walked away for a moment, staring into the darkening night. He went to where the sports car was stuck in the sand, getting a good look at how deep the tires had dug themselves into the loose sand. The car wasn't going anywhere. There was always the chance that he could use the cruiser to drag it out of the wash, but he decided against it.

With the guys still cuffed he had to lift their pants back up for them, not wanting to risk a fight with the men unshackled.

"Ok, you two, into the back of the cruiser." He opened the door behind the driver's side and motioned for them to get in.

"You're not going to read us our rights?" Alastair said, coyly.

The Billy looked him up and down. "After the stunt you two pulled, you know damned well what's coming next. Get in the car!"

Ben and Alastair snickered to themselves. It might have been new territory for Ben, but Alastair knew damned well how the Billys would always act like nothing had happened. No matter how quickly they were willing to drop their "professional demeanor" they always went straight back to the macho "nothing to see here" look that cops wore so well.

The cruiser pulled out of the wash and drove at a reasonable speed back toward the highway. The cruiser rattled on the washboarded road, but the vibration wasn't as severe at such a reduced speed. From the back of the cab they watched as the sports car was engulfed in darkness and left there to rot.

$$\text{❧} \quad 8 \quad \text{☙}$$

Back in the city they were booked, the whole thing, just business as usual. All along the ride back the Billy had said nothing to them. Several times he had said something into the radio but Alastair and Ben couldn't hear any of it through the plexiglass divider. Once back on the freeway he had picked up speed, driving way over the limit. But still it had taken nearly an hour to get to the station.

The Billy left them at the booking counter and disappeared down the hallway.

"You think we'll see him again?" Ben asked Alastair in a hushed voice.

Alastair didn't even try to contain his laughter. "There's a lot of 'him.' Back home we made a game of checking out the badge numbers and..."

Before he could finish the officer behind the counter stamped their papers and called for another officer to take them away. A big burly cop came and took them both by the cuffs to lead them off to the holding cell. Neither of them had even bothered to listen to the charges. They'd find out soon enough.

As they were led down the hall past the drunk tanks and processing cells men shouted at them, many hooting and hollering. A proper jail welcome. Once at the end of the hall the cop unlocked and slid open the cell door and pushed them both inside. Once inside both of them backed up to the bars to allow the officer to remove the cuffs. Both of them knew the drill well, and this wasn't missed on the cop.

The officer's boots echoed down the hallway as he walked away. The shouting had stopped now that the excitement was over. It was only then that Alastair and Ben turned to see who their cellmates were.

"Well, I'll be damned! Is that you, Diego?" There was genuine surprise in Alastair's voice.

The look on Diego's face was priceless. "Alastair? What are you doing here?"

"I'll give you one guess." Alastair shook his head, not bothering to provide the obvious answer. "Hey, Diego. Meet Slapjack."

The men shook hands and looked each other up and down. The other guys in the holding cell looked the other way and stayed out of the conversation. Ben took a seat and left the guys to it.

"Wasn't sure that you got away. Guess you sure did, though. You left town to escape the heat too, I suppose you did." Alastair wasn't going to bother with what would presumably be Diego's long-winded story. "I don't think Jacky was so lucky. Never did hear from him again. Fucking Golden Goose, slipped right through our fingers..."

Diego cut in, "They got Billys here." He said it like a revelation.

"Oh, they sure do. Got real familiar with one on the way here. Highway Patrol, that's something different." Alastair snickered.

"Word on the streets is that they are trying out something different here. Back home shit was caving in on itself. Heat was on for sure. I got pulled in and questioned. Didn't say shit." For as dumb as Diego could be, he was no rat.

Alastair patted him on the shoulder in approval. "Yeah, the program was dealt a major blow. But they ain't going to give up on their investment so easily. You notice any difference with the Billys out here? They seem a little different."

"The uniforms are different. Haven't seen any on the beat."

"Yeah, no shit. I mean about them, how they act." Alastair was already losing his patience with Diego's dimness.

It went right over Diego's head. "Yeah, yeah, they do act a little differently. More standoffish. I've only nailed one, so far. But he was raw and rough. Didn't beat around the bush. Not too friendly either. But... Still hot as fuck and ready to ride. Word on the streets is that these guys are tough as nails."

"Think they ramped up the supercop angle?" Alastair didn't wait for an answer and provided his own, "I'll bet they learned a few things back home. Keeping these guys on the road and off of the streets had to be on purpose. With the stain we gave'um they probably had to change it up." Alastair smirked, remembering all those notches in his belt.

"I haven't heard much talk about them. They must be keeping it low-pro." Diego, shifty as ever, glanced around the cell to see who was listening.

Alastair grabbed his face and turned it toward him. "Have the cruisers caught on yet? What kind of competition are we looking at?"

Diego swatted Alastair's hand away. "I don't think so. Like I said, not much talk on the street. But I haven't been around here too long. Plus, no way to draw'um out unless you're on the road. Lot of guys on the streets got no ride."

Ben was staring at them, perched on the edge of a bunk. He had wisely claimed one for himself as soon as the gate clicked shut. The other bunks were all occupied already. Alastair knew the drill, but the surprise of seeing Diego had distracted him from thinking straight.

"You been in here long?" Alastair now spoke in a hushed tone. The other guys in the cell were paying more attention to them now, and he didn't like the looks of them.

Diego seemed oblivious to the other guys in the cell, other than Ben, who he couldn't stop eyeing. "A couple days, I think. They nabbed me for walking out of a restaurant without paying. Of all the things to get pinched for... Hey, what happened to Jacky?"

"That night, you must have heard it, there was gun fire. Pretty sure that the Golden Goose got him. I had to bail in a hurry. He wasn't behind me. I never saw him again." Alastair looked down at his feet. It hadn't been his fault but he never could stomach one of the guys getting ghosted on his watch.

Diego's eyes were wide. "You mean you guys didn't get the Golden Goose?"

"Barely even saw him. He was packing heat, we should have known. Didn't you catch any of the news after we split? You must have come out here to get away from it, right?" Alastair was getting impatient. As usual, Diego didn't know shit.

Oblivious, Diego kept talking, "What's the deal with your friend over there? You got a new crew already? He looks tasty."

Before Alastair could answer, a uniformed officer banged on the bars with his nightstick. "You. And you. Come with me." He pointed to Ben and Alastair.

Diego looked confused. So did the guys, but they obeyed and backed up to the bars again, awaiting cuffs. The cop laughed and gave the bars another good whack.

"That won't be necessary. Out, get on with it." He waited for them to start down the hallway, following closely behind. Ben started to mouth a question and was quickly told to buckle it. Once they were back to the booking area the cop spoke up again, "Ok, you're free to go. Go on, get out of here. And don't let me see you around again."

Alastair and Ben looked at each other in disbelief. They'd barely been in for a few hours. Alastair spoke up, "Someone bailed us out?" He couldn't imagine who that 'someone' could have been. He didn't know anyone in town except for Ben.

The cop looked at him disapprovingly. "Bail? No, you've been discharged. No charges were pressed. Now, you gonna get out of here or what?"

They didn't wait for any further explanation. It was time to go. Without looking back they fast-walked down the hall to the exit, passing cops and their prey along the way, avoiding eye contact as much as possible.

The door to the station swung open and bathed them in harsh sunlight. They must have been in through the whole night without noticing the time pass. The shock of seeing Diego had disoriented him. They took off heading east, putting as much distance between them and the station as possible while trying not to look suspicious. Neither of them spoke until they were several blocks away.

"What the fuck was that? No charges? They had us red handed." Ben nodded his head as Alastair spoke. It didn't make any sense to him either.

Ben straightened himself up, feeling more confident now that they were away from the station. "That Billy, he must have taken a liking to us or something. Never heard of being brought in for grand theft auto and being released. What are we, fish? Catch and release?"

It didn't make sense unless the Billy was afraid of being caught too. Maybe they were being extra cautious because of what had happened after the scandals. But a slap on the wrist, it was insane. Neither of them could believe that freedom would come so soon. Why book them at all? Was it just to send a message?

"Fuck it. Were out. And glad of it. What now?" Alastair looked at Ben. Despite all the excitement, he had no idea where to go or what to do. The city was still unfamiliar, and making less sense the more time he spent here.

Ben didn't suffer the same confusion. Nor did he seem to care why they had been released, only that they were free now. "Wanna go for a ride?"

"Are you kidding? We're only three blocks from the station. And we've got no wheels."

"You got a better idea? I figure we should put as many miles between us and the copshop as we can, and quick. You feel like sticking around, or something?" Ben had picked up his pace and was eyeing every parked car that they passed.

He had a point, but the car game wasn't so engrained in Alastair's repertoire. He was distracted trying to figure out what the Billy had been up to. For as many as he'd laid, once they threw you in a cell they usually didn't let you out so easy.

"All right. Let's get the fuck out of here. I'm gonna need some rest, or at least a drink, and soon." He caved to Ben's confidence.

Ben smirked. "And what about your friend, Diego?"

"Fuck him. Ain't nothing we could do for him anyway. But seriously, he's still in there for nothing but a dine and dash, and we're walking free. It doesn't make sense. We..." The words died on his lips as he saw Ben make his move.

"This one'll do nicely." Ben straddled a motorcycle that was parked at the curb. "Come on. Room for two. Get on. What are you waiting for?"

Alastair threw his leg over the bike and scooched up against Ben's back as he fiddled with the ignition and worked his magic. The hog roared to life, spraying out exhaust and filling the street with revving sounds. Ben didn't bother with being subtle. He flipped the kickstand and kept revving the engine.

"Any particular destination?" He didn't wait for an answer and pulled out into the street, accelerating as if he didn't want anything other than to see how fast the bike could go. He wouldn't have been able to hear Alastair's response over the engine noise anyway.

They sped down the street, doubling back and passing the police station. A line of police bikes sat inert in the parking lot and they zoomed past without incident, despite the volume of the bike tearing through the stiflingly hot city air. Without helmets the wind blew through their hair and a great sense of freedom ran through them. Not just the freedom of being out of the jail and back on the streets, but the immense freedom of mobility.

Ben took turn after turn, ignoring the red lights and barely decelerating while taking the corners. Other motorists honked as they passed but Ben merely swerved out of the way and cut lanes to pass them. Alastair wrapped his arms tightly around Ben's midsection, holding on for dear life as Ben pushed the bike even faster. With their bodies pressed so close together he could feel both of their hearts pounding with exhilaration. The harder he squeezed the faster Ben drove, testing the limits of the bike as the city streets ripped behind them.

As Ben sent the bike barreling between the lines of cars waiting at a red light they passed a patrol car on their right. The familiar warning siren blazed but Ben paid no mind and raced on. They left the police car in the dust, too blocked in by the traffic to pursue. Alastair erupted with laughter as he looked back and caught the officer's frustrated face, impotent to do anything but wait for the traffic to clear and the light to change. Ben yanked the throttle and squeezed every last bit of power from the motorcycle.

Ben yelled over the sound of the bike, "The freeway is up there. Want to see what this ride can really do?"

He didn't wait for an answer and weaved through the thick line of cars toward the onramp. He got on the freeway heading west, out of the city. Traffic was also thick on the overpass but he deftly drove between the lines of cars swerving to avoid the vehicles changing lanes. The further they got from the city the more the road opened up, and the harder he pushed the engine. Alastair loosened his grip and let himself relax into the speed.

Ben was intent on the road, barely noticing that Alastair had freed his hands from around him. Alastair leaned back and unclasped his belt and lowered the zipper on his pants. His cock stirred with the exhilaration of the ride. He pulled it free and it spring up and out of his pants, now feeling the freedom of the hot wind along with the rest of him. Again, he reached around Ben and loosened his belt as well. Ben didn't look back but understood what he was doing and raised his body off of the bike to allow Alastair to yank his pants down just enough to expose his rear.

Now both partially nude they continued to speed down the highway. Alastair spit in his hand and rubbed the spittle onto the head of his cock. Ben didn't waste any time taking the cue and lowered himself onto Alastair, moving back and forth to adjust and find the right angle, all the while steering the bike toward the horizon.

Ninety miles an hour, one hundred. He bobbed up and down on Alastair's lap matching the speed of the bike to the rhythm of Alastair thrusting his pelvis up into Ben's raised body. They were barely paying attention to the road.

Two motorcycle cops wove through the traffic behind them, having received an APB on a reckless biker. They had to cut lanes to catch up, riding as dangerously as the cycle they pursued. Their sirens blared over the sounds of the freeway and they shouted into their loud-speakers for drivers to get out of the way and pull into the slower lanes.

Ben noticed them in the rearview mirror and cranked the bike into higher gear, continuing to raise and lower himself onto Alastair. He brought the bike up to one hundred and ten. Officers Troy and Jernigan tried to match their speed and started to close the distance between them. Once they were close enough to catch the view of what was happening on the other bike they both looked over at each other in amazement. Ben picked up even more speed and pulled around to the front a semi, blocking the officers' view for a moment as they cut across the divider and pulled a high-speed U-ey to the other side of the freeway. They were barreling in the other direction before the cops could even notice and try to correct. They were more than a mile behind before they gained sight of them and attempted to catch up. Alastair would have blown his load a long time ago if he hadn't came so many times over the last few days, and Ben just kept on pushing himself up and down onto Alastair's rock-hard dick.

Shouting over the road noise into his headset Officer Jernigan addressed Troy, "They're going nearly a hundred and twenty, do you think we should call in backup?"

Officer Troy looked over at Jernigan to his left and shook his head. "These ones are ours. Let's see what these bikes can do."

They both accelerated, and as they tried to close the gap Troy's cock began to stir with the thrill of the chase. He wasn't close enough to catch a good look at Jernigan, but figured that under the hood he was facing similar arousal. He veered closer, hoping to see if he was correct, but he had to focus his eyes on the road to handle the speed of the cars rushing up at them. They both gunned it as the space between them and their prey grew with the potential of losing them.

Up ahead Ben and Alastair pumped away and brought the bike to its limits. In the throes of fucking they had forgotten all about the cops in pursuit. Nothing existed except for them and the road, speed, and the wind in their hair. The bike topped off at one hundred and thirty-six miles an hour, whining in protest as it reached top speed. Alastair couldn't hold it anymore and blew hard inside of Ben, who, in the thrill of the chase, continued to raise and lower his body onto Alastair's softening cock. Alastair slapped his ass and lifted if off of him; he couldn't stand another moment of it. Even though he was starting to stiffen again, there was nothing left in him and it was taking all of his strength to steady himself on the back of the bike.

Ben lifted himself off of Alastair and moved to sit back down on the seat. Hot jizz leaked out of him as Alastair pulled at his pants trying to get them back up. They continued at breakneck speed, leaving the cops in the dust as they wove through the cars, lengthening the distance between them with every second. Once the fuzz had disappeared from the mirrors Ben took the next exit and continued though the streets. He brought the bike back down to a reasonable speed and the engine now purred with the comfort of a lower gear.

"Did we leave the Billys in the dust, or what?" Ben said over his shoulder.

Alastair was having a difficult time keeping himself from giddy laughter. "Those weren't Billys. Not even Highway Patrol. Their bikes weren't fast enough."

❧ 10 ❧

Officers Troy and Jernigan veered back and forth across the lanes in search of the fugitives but saw no sign of any other motorcycles. They had been shamelessly left behind on a road that no longer felt like theirs. But the thrill of the chase had left them both eager for more – speed, high adrenaline, action. Even just having his ass on the leather seat was tempting Troy with an indescribable urge. A need. He wondered if Jernigan was feeling it too.

Officer Jernigan signaled with his hand for Troy to take the next exit with him. They pulled off of the highway into an industrial neighborhood. Both sides of the street were lined with work vehicles, but no pedestrians were in sight. Warehouses dotted the landscape and the asphalt was hot enough to cook on. Only at lowered speeds could they feel the stifling pressure of the desert heat. Troy's heart still pumped hard from the excitement of driving so fast and he couldn't keep himself from grinning. It was the fastest he had ever driven and he wondered if it was the same for Jernigan. They had been partners on the force for only a few months, and this had been their first chase, albeit an unsuccessful one. Still, there was something deeply satisfying about taking the bikes to their limits. He wasn't finished.

Troy followed Jernigan down the endless streets, knowing that they had long since stopped looking for the suspects. Jernigan was looking for something else. And he wasn't letting on what. They moved past warehouse after warehouse, heading deeper into the industrial areas of the city. Some of the warehouses were now being replaced by factories, making everything from cement to God knows what. Jernigan downshifted and slowly brought the bike to the curb. He lifted his leg over the motorcycle and kicked it into place at the side of the road. Officer Troy followed suit.

Without a word Jernigan set off walking toward the alley that led around to the back of the massive industrial building. Troy followed unquestioningly, still not coming down from the chase. Every step rubbed his uniform against his still hard cock. He took it in his hand through his pants, not wanting the erection to fade. Up ahead Jernigan's cuffs jingled with every step until he came to the back of the building. He stopped in his tracks and looked to the left and right. Not seeing anyone, he leaned forward against the wall and dropped trou. His nightstick, gun, and cuffs clanked against the pavement around his boots. Troy didn't need any coaxing and took the hint.

Not even bothering to look around Troy undid his pants and pulled his still hard dick out. Officer Jernigan spread his legs wider and propped himself up with hands on the wall. He brought one to his lips and licked across the palm and fingers, making sure to leave a thick trail of saliva. He ran his hand between his ass cheeks and used the same hand to spread himself in invitation.

Troy moved up against him and slowly let himself in, letting Jernigan take a moment to open himself up. He slid in inch by inch, moving past the head until the shaft was fully inside. Once he was in to the hilt he moved himself back out, still moving slowly and waiting for Jernigan to fully open. Once he sensed the loosening he quickened his pace and started thrusting with vigor. All the while scenes from the chase ran through his mind. The speed. The cars flying by. And the road racing beneath them. He imagined that Jernigan was thinking much the same. Troy threw his head back and forgot all about the road, losing himself in the ecstasy of finally being inside his partner. For as many times as he had thought of it, he had figured that Jernigan would never go for it. Now, he was riding him as if he was a favorite bike, intimately familiar, built for speed and prowess. Jernigan reached back and cupped Troy's ass, pulling him further in and with greater speed. Troy could barely handle it but held on as best he could. To distract himself from cumming he reached around and took Jernigan's cock in his hand, working it at the same pace as his pumping. When he felt Jernigan's balls tightening he let himself go, and as Officer Jernigan spurt his load onto the wall in front of him, Troy also let go and spilled himself into his partner.

Ben and Alastair rolled back into the main drag after ditching the motorcycle in an alley. As nice as the bike was, it was too hot to keep riding. They walked several blocks and found themselves back at the bar where they had met. Ben ordered beers for them while Alastair found a dark booth in the back of the room. He hadn't slept in too long, but the adrenaline of the chase was still surging through him and he doubted he'd be able to sleep even if the booth had been a king-sized bed.

Ben sat down and placed the pints in front of them. Alastair raised his glass to cheers. "You are one crazy motherfucker. To speed!"

Their glasses clinked and they both slugged down the cool frothy beers, each draining half the glass in one pull. They drank the rest in silence before Alastair went up to the bar for refills. As he waited for the barkeep he felt a tap on his shoulder.

"So, we meet again." It was Diego.

Alastair slapped him on the back. "No shit. So, they let you out after all. And you found our place, huh?"

Diego nodded. "Yeah. It's no secret. Lots of the guys on the street haunt this place. Cheap beer too." He ordered himself a round as well and looked over to where

Ben was sitting. "I see you're still rolling around with your friend."

Alastair ignored the comment about Ben. "What have you been doing other than sitting around waiting to be released? Any more word on the Billys?"

Wiping suds away from his mouth Diego said, "Well, I was holed up in there for a while. Ended up letting me off with a fine. But when I finally got out La Migra was waiting for me outside. Thought I was toast for a minute." He took another pull. "Those assholes looked mean, too. Shook me down. Masked fuckers. Didn't even ask questions about where I was from, they just dragged me behind the station and for a minute, I figured I was a goner."

"Hold on a second." Alastair took one of the pints over to Ben, knowing that it wouldn't stay cold for long. He returned to the bar and nodded at Diego to continue.

Diego ordered another round for both of them, neglecting to order one for Ben. "When they brought me to the back of the building there was an unmarked van there. Like they were going to disappear me or something. And when they shoved me in back I thought that that was that. But these guys, they both got in back with me too. Didn't flash badges or anything and I started to wonder if they were really La Migra or what."

Alastair was shaking his head like he didn't believe a word Diego was saying. But either Diego didn't notice or didn't care. He glanced over at Ben, but he didn't look like he was going anywhere and wasn't paying any attention to them anyway.

"These guys, they took turns on me like they had been pent up for years. They each took more than one round, too. And when I thought that they were through, each of them splayed himself out for me to take a turn. And shit, these Migra guys, oh boy were they willing. Almost as good as Billy ass, if you ask me."

"I didn't. But they let you go after that?"

"Yep. First, they drove me a few blocks away, and I figured I was done for. Then they pulled over and told me to get out. Just like that. They dropped me off here, can you believe that?"

Alastair kept shaking his head. "So, they're onto this place?"

"Shit, Alastair, it's just a bar. Hell, they probably drink here too." Diego finished the last of his second beer and tapped the counter to signal for another.

"And the Billys? You hear any more about them?" Alastair was eager to return to the booth with Ben, but Diego didn't look like he wanted to leave his barstool.

"Oh yeah. Like I said before, they're only on the highways, so I haven't heard too many of the guys talking about them. Probably hasn't caught on yet. And apparently, if you're into uniforms, there's options. But I did hear something that might interest you."

It was always annoying how Diego drew things out, taking his time to deliver. "Yeah, what's that?" The impatience in Alastair's voice was obvious to anyone who was actually listening, but Diego didn't seem to notice.

"The Billys, well, they're still pretty new here. And apparently not everyone wants them here after what happened back home. But...there's a conference coming up, some big Cops of the Future thing. Introducing them to the regular force, or something. I saw a pamphlet on the bulletin board while I was getting booked." Trying to build up momentum for his story he paused for a while.

Alastair didn't want to take the bait but was eager to hear what he was going on about. "Yeah, get it out."

The irritation went over Diego's head. "Well, the pamphlet said that the Golden Goose is going to be at the convention, keynote speaker, or something like that. I guess they're bringing him in to try and convince the local cops that the Billys would be a good thing for the city."

So, they would have another shot at the Golden Goose. Dale Thompson was going to be in town and away from his family. Apparently, the scandal hadn't hit as hard across state lines. He'd be talking to a whole room full of cops. And who knew how many Billys might be there. And Alastair wasn't about to let Diego fuck this one up. He might need him as a distraction again, but the Golden Goose was his. Maybe Ben could take a turn too, but he didn't seem as interested in the Billys. Alastair was ready for another notch.

+ 12 +

Intentionally walking up the street to the copshop never felt like a good idea. But Alastair had to get his hands on one of those pamphlets. Maybe what Diego said had been true, but he had to see for himself. For all he knew the convention was taking place back in California and Diego had no idea what he was talking about. Beat cops and plainclothes officers were everywhere, and many of them eyed Alastair suspiciously. Not a Highway Patrol officer in sight, but that probably wasn't unusual since their office was a few miles away. Alastair wondered how much contact the two departments had, or if relations were strained, in the way the firemen and cops didn't get on well. If such a rivalry existed, then the introduction of Billys to the force couldn't be going over very well. Perhaps that was the whole point of the conference.

Hands in his pockets, he strutted up the street trying to look nonchalant. He made sure that his pace wasn't too fast or too slow, nothing to draw more attention than he was already getting. Typically, these were the kinds of places that he was being dragged into, not stopping by on his own volition. He came up to the stairs, hesitated for a moment, and ascended, hoping that a bulletin board might be located just on the other side of the doors.

It felt strange to be walking in a free man. Inside the station the place was abuzz with activity. Men being booked, cops on their way in and out, and the crackle of radios dispatching men to action all over the city. Once inside, no one paid him much mind, as if they all knew that walk-ins would probably cause more unnecessary work for them. Everyone looked busy, and everywhere he looked there was a flurry of activity. He tried not to make eye contact, instead keeping his gaze at crotch level to the officers. They usually liked this sign of submission.

Alastair didn't want to ask any questions, even for directions, but wasn't seeing any bulletin board or a place for announcements. Behind the glass, officers and secretaries worked at computers, few turning their eyes up at an approaching visitor. Those who did see him looked suspicious at his approach, but their eyes fell away when he didn't look back and just kept moving.

There were only so many places to look without having to move through doors or into a room where he knew he would be unwelcome and would have to answer to his presence. To the right he saw the elevators and moved toward them in hopes that there would be a directory nearby. He'd been in the building before, but the action of being booked had prevented him from taking in the scenery or trying to commit the layout to memory. Something to keep in mind for next time, whenever that occurred.

As he took the corner leading to the elevators, he found what he was looking for. The bulletin board was filled with wanted posters and various announcements. Alastair scanned the faces on the posters and breathed a sigh of relief that his face wasn't among those being hunted. Some of the guys looked familiar, but the streets of this city were still new to him, and he hadn't quite made the rounds enough to be familiar with the urchins.

In the center of the corkboard he found it. In bright blue letters the header announced the Cops of the Future program being integrated throughout the city. Below the words a pristine photo of a smiling Billy, looking both tough and friendly at the same time. This was it. But he didn't want to linger in the station any longer than he had to. Looking both ways to see if he was being watched, and confirming that everyone in the halls were too busy to pay him any mind, he reached up and yanked the pamphlet from the thumbtack and shoved it in his pocket. He lingered for a moment longer pretending to peruse the announcements then turned on his heels and headed for the exit, keeping his head down and doing his best to look like his business here was through.

In the corner of his eye, he thought he recognized the motorcycle cops from the freeway, but knew better than to take a second look and provoke their curiosity. The huge doors swinging closed behind him was a relief. At the same time the heat hit him in full force. He had been so determined to find the announcement that he hadn't even noticed how luxuriously cold the cops kept the station. Tax dollars at work.

He took the stairs two at a time on his way down and blended back into the anonymity of the streets as quickly as he could. What was it about cops that evoked such fear and excitement at the same time? Just the thought of it made him rise, but there would be time for that later. Preferably with some degree of privacy and without the whole damn force on his back.

It had been days since he had slept, and he was starting to feel it. Adrenaline could only prop him up for so long. And the heat of the day wasn't helping. Neither side of the street provided any shade and he felt the overwhelming desire to be indoors, preferably alone, catching a bit of well needed rest.

Up ahead he saw a cheap motel, the kind where pros hung around by the ice machines, and figured that this place was as good as any. It would cost him his last sixty bucks, but that was the least of his concerns at the moment. There was always more money somewhere and he'd find it when he needed it. At least here no one would bother him, and from the looks of those milling around, he wasn't going to stick out much.

Alastair threw the keys onto the nightstand, drew the blinds, and turned the TV on with the volume down. The queen size bed was rickety. He figured he'd have to sleep on top of the covers rather than risk seeing what the sheets looked like, but none of that mattered; he was too tired to care. A bit of privacy was also a welcome change.

He unwrapped the little bar of soap that smelled like cheap perfume and stepped into his first shower in days. The pressure was weak, and the water only got lukewarm, but he stood there letting himself soak for nearly twenty minutes. Every time the room next door flushed the toilet the pressure would drop even further, and for some reason they were using the bathroom multiple times while he was rinsing off. But small comforts outweighed the annoyance, and he tried not to think about it while he washed his hair.

There were no full-sized towels, so he dried off with the washcloths that had been left on the rack, at least they looked somewhat clean. Still naked, he sat down in front of the TV and zoned out for a while. Nothing interesting flashed across the screen and he couldn't find any news programs to see if the recent chases were being talked about. Nothing about the Cops of the Future program event either. Maybe the city was trying to play it safe and ease the Billys onto the force before trying to get the public on their side. They wouldn't have an easy time of it if anyone around here had been paying attention to the news coming out of California. But for all he knew, all that had blown over as well.

So, they were being cautious. There was something about that that didn't add up. He got up and retrieved the pamphlet from the nightstand where he'd thrown the rest of his things. He sat back down on the same spot and leafed through it. It was all pretty much as Diego had said. Apparently, he had been right about something for once in his life. Law enforcement from all departments all over the city would be meeting at the convention center for presentations about the Billys. The pamphlet made the whole thing look pretty slick: crime rate statistics, the benefits of an enlarged force, regular cops' lives protected, and the track records of other Billy programs that had been enacted around the country. So, the Cops of the Future program had gone nationwide, or was at least starting to, city by city.

On the back page was a list of speakers and presenters above the schedule for the event. And sure enough, Dale Thompson was on top of the list, accolades listed next to his name. The guy had received a lot of medals from his time on the force; it was obvious why they had chosen him as Model 0 for the program, and it wasn't just for his good looks and hot bod. Alastair wondered if there were Billys made from the genetics of other cops too.

Bored of the interior details of the pamphlet he folded it back up and flipped to the front cover. Surrounded in a corporate blue frame was a full body shot of one of the Billys stepping out of a patrol car. His hand rested on top of the door and the other arm looked like it was reaching for something. The shot had been set up to look like the Billy was about to burst into action, but it could also be interpreted as a friendly gesture. Whoever had set up the shot was thinking about multiple angles of public perception. And Alastair was thinking of yet another.

Still naked, his cock began to rise, thinking of all those Billys from the past and the future. He squinted his eyes and tried to think of the Billy in the picture as a little older, as Dale Thompson, the Golden Goose. It wasn't hard to imagine his face, as he had seen it before, both on television, and in the family photos lining his hallways. He pushed the thought of the Golden Goose's house out of his mind and brought his focus back onto the picture on the pamphlet. He took himself in his hand and started working slowly, first focusing on that chiseled face and then thinking about stripping off that uniform and everything that was underneath.

His cock grew rock hard as he moved with it. Every Billy he had ever fucked blew threw his mind, notch after notch, in the backs of patrol cars, in the alleys, in the bars, every thrust and slurp of jizz he had shared with them. On the TV in front of him the screen showed a commercial for a sports car racing through the mountains and on the coast, always free from traffic and ready for speed. Instead of distracting him it made him swell even more, and he slowed down for a minute, not wanting to cum just yet. The TV went back to some sitcom and he refocused his attention to the Bil-ly's face, his pressed uniform, and those long legs prop-ping him up.

He laid down on his side, the pamphlet in his free hand, and continued to stroke himself. He imagined all of the Billys lined up, each waiting for their turn as he worked his way through the line, giving and taking, his appetite growing with each progressive fuck. He imagined Dale Thompson at the end of the line, waiting and watching, fondling the Billy in front of him in anticipation. He would try to hold it until he reached the Golden Goose, but all that fine ass on the way was making it difficult. His mind raced to the front of the line, and he took Dale's cock into his hand, seeing that he was even bigger than the Billys in front of him. He looked into Dale's eyes and motioned for him to turn around, one look at his ass all pent up, he shot hot loads of cum on to the Billy's face on the front of the brochure. The cum seeped into the paper and the soiled pamphlet wrinkled up, while Alastair let his head fall to the pillow and drifted off to sleep.

$$\clubsuit \quad 14 \quad \clubsuit$$

Feeling fresher than he had since arriving in Arizona he strolled out of the room and dropped the keys in the box by the window. He was still getting used to the geography of the city with its long endless streets marking out a grid, crisscrossed with highways. It wasn't a great place for walking, nor did he feel like it; the sun was already starting to cook the streets. They would be needing a plan to get into the convention, but first he would have to find the guys. It would be crazy to try and get into a place with that many cops, and Alastair would need all the help he could get just to get inside unnoticed. But that would have to wait. First a ride.

He continued walking away from the motel, figuring that nabbing a car from the parking lot would be too likely to implicate him. This run-down part of town didn't have much in the way of luxury vehicles, and he wasn't about to risk getting pinched for a beater, not with the convention coming up so soon. Despite it being morning he was already sweating like crazy. His thoughts went to AC and cold beer.

Alastair loathed the idea of riding public transit, but when he came upon a bus stop, he figured that catching a lift closer to the nice neighborhoods, where the nicer cars would be, would save him having to walk through the heat. At least the bench was shaded. He fumbled with the last of the change in his pocket and counted out just enough for the ride. Pulling a crumpled pack of smokes from his shirt pocket he lit one in hopes that smoking a cigarette would call the bus into existence and it would show up before he could even smoke half. It almost always worked.

Sure enough, after a few drags the bus screeched up to the stop and the door swung open. A cool blast of air met his face as he stepped inside. Now all he needed was that beer. The bus wasn't too crowded. People sat several seats away from each other, intentionally avoiding having to sit near their neighbors. Alastair strolled past them to the back, grabbing the ceiling rail to avoid stumbling as the bus pulled back into traffic and toward the heart of the city.

On the bench in the back sat one lone man. He stared out the window and didn't bother to look at Alastair as he sat down on the bench near him, just a seat away. The man looked like a tough guy, leather pants, tight shirt, knife on his belt. He could almost be a cop, but he wore the look of the streets about him. Alastair scooched over to the seat next to him.

"You know how long this bus takes to get to the main drag?" It was a question, but Alastair framed it more like a hello.

For the first time the guy looked over at him and without smiling said, "Who's asking?"

Alastair laughed. He knew the routine. And the guy was handsome. "Name's Alastair." He started to move back a seat, but the man grabbed him by the wrist and kept him where he was.

"New around here. Are you?" It directly translated into 'fresh meat.'

Not bothering to answer, Alastair pulled at the man's belt, loosening the buckle right next to the knife. While he did this the guy followed suit and did the same with Alastair's pants. Not even bothering to look up at the other passengers both of them freed their cocks from their pants and started to stroke each other off. Out the window the city smeared by in a blur as the bus barreled down the road.

They both moved at the same rhythm. The guy's dick had so much girth that Alastair could barely wrap his fingers around the whole thing, which only made his dick even harder. The guy knew that he was packing heat and grinned at Alastair. He sped up his rhythm, nearly bringing Alastair to climax, and then slowed down again, not letting him finish yet. The tease made him even harder, and in his hand Alastair could feel the guy throb, each stroke bringing him closer to cumming. Alastair sped up to match the pulse. He looked at the man in the eyes and could tell that he was getting close by the way his lids started to droop. Looking past the guy, out the window he saw that they had entered a familiar part of the city. They were just blocks from the bar where the guys usually hung out. Never letting go of the man's cock he reached up and pulled the cord with his free hand.

As the bus started to pull up to the curb Alastair knew that he wouldn't have time to finish. But he quickly got on his knees between the seats and took the man in his mouth as best he could. He could barely wrap his lips around the bulk of the cock, but he tried his best and moved his tongue quickly around the head, driving the man closer to orgasm. He felt the bus come to a stop and knew he was running out of time. He opened his mouth as wide as he could and took the dick in as deep as possible. The guy reached up and held Alastair's head in place, unloading as he did so. Alastair tasted the hot salty flood on his tongue and swallowed as he stood up.

He put his junk back into his pants as he ran to the bus door, barely making it before it swung shut. He was still hard as fuck and would need to find a finish soon.

He jumped to the curb and saw the guy looking at him through the window as the bus pulled away. Gazing down the street he saw that he was only a block away from the bar and the cold beer he'd been wanting.

$$\maltese \quad 15 \quad \maltese$$

"Look at you, looking all clean-cut." Shouted Diego from the bar.

"Oh, shut up! What have you bums been up to?" Alastair took a seat in between Diego and Ben. He didn't have any interest in discussing the details of what he had been up to since seeing them last.

Ben slapped him on the back and slid a pint over to him. Alastair took a long slug, draining most of the glass. Between gulps he tapped on the bar for another. "You're buying, right?" He looked over to Ben, who nodded his head reluctantly, and then looked at Diego suggesting that he help out with the drinks. If the place had been more packed Diego would probably be lolly-gagging his beers already.

Diego seemed to miss the cue and chimed in, "You all see the news about all the carjackings and grand theft auto? Figured you guys might know something about that. Could bring out the Billys in full force..."

"What is it with you guys and these Billys? Seriously, y'all have one track minds for those guys." Said Ben.

"If you don't get it, you probably never will." Said Alastair over the rim of his glass. "But you've seen them, I'll give you one guess. What do you think we see in them?"

"Yeah, yeah, I get it, they're hot. But that's all you two ever talk about, like it's some secret club or something."

Alastair and Diego gave each other a knowing look.

Ben continued, "I mean, I get the uniform thing, but really, what's the big deal? Cops. No one like cops."

All three of them started laughing. Ben had a point about that. But the Billys were no ordinary cops. It was hard to believe that anybody wouldn't see it for themselves.

Alastair stopped laughing and changed the tone, "Of all people, I'd think you'd get it. And you will if you hear me out. Look, guys, that convention that Diego was talking about is on. And it's tomorrow. I need you guys to help me find a way in. The place is going to be crawling with the fuzz. Billys too. We need to get in there. And... the Golden Goose is going to be there too. This is our chance.

They filled Ben in on Dale Thompson and their thwarted goals a few months back. They told him all about the Billy Club, too. Ben's eyes widened in recognition as their point started to sink in. It might not be fully his thing, but he got it. And he had to admit, it sounded like a challenge. Something different, at least.

Ben cut them off, "So, what you're saying is that you want the three of us to infiltrate this Cops of the Future seminar. And then what?"

Alastair slammed his empty pint on the counter. "And then what? Haven't you been listening. Then we get to the Golden Goose! Not to mention a limitless supply of Billys. The regular cops might not like them, but so far they have been... receptive, to say the least." He motioned to the barkeep for another. "If you had seen what happened in California, you'd be rooting for this to happen. The force nearly fell apart from the scandal. So many layers of fun, you wouldn't believe it. Now we have the chance to do it all over again. Do you have any idea how much these guys must have spent on this program? And we have the chance to fuck it all up, no pun intended."

Ben was slowly nodding his head. Sure, the Billys were hot. But there was more to this plan. And knowing that, he could get fully behind it. Why not stir things up in the city? The more the cops fought amongst themselves, or looked bad in the public eye, the more freedom they'd have on the streets. At least for a while.

Diego pulled a wrinkled pamphlet from his back pocket and showed it to Ben. As he looked it over it all started to make sense. It would be risky as hell walking right into the lion's den, but no one would ever suspect that anyone would have the balls to do so. The element of surprise could go a long way.

The three of them sat in silence for a while, thinking. They ordered another round and went out back to smoke and bounce ideas around. Stealing uniforms? No, that would be too much of a risk, kidnapping officers would get them put away for good. Acting like concerned citizens? Folks would take one look at them and know it was bullshit. Pretending to be from a human rights group? That was even more laughable than acting like people from the neighborhood. They batted a bunch of ideas around but nothing was sticking.

They chain smoked in silence for a while, sweating as the sun rose higher in the air and the shade from the surrounding umbrellas evaporated.

Ben looked at the picture of the Billy on the cover of the pamphlet. "Yeah, I can see it now. I get it. The guy that took us in, he was one of these guys?"

Alastair looked at the picture and then back to Ben. "Yep. That's the one. Or rather, he was one of them."

"And all of that really went down in Cali?"

Alastair nodded. "Every word of it is true. They were easier to keep track of with street cop badge numbers. But you get the gist. There's so many of them now... it's a feast. We thought we had it made with a hundred of them."

"And now they're rolling out the program all over the country?" Ben looked incredulous.

Alastair laughed. "That looks like the plan. But... we could have an impact on what happens next."

Diego started to say something but Ben cut him off. "So, if you're so into these guys, these Billys, why would you want to get the program canceled?"

Again, Alastair laughed. "Don't you see? These guys might be fuckable, but they're still cops. We can have the best of both worlds. Fuck tha police, you know? Have our cake and eat it too."

Ben looked at him with a spreading recognition. This wasn't just about sticking it to the *Man*, it was *sticking* it to the Man! It was all making sense now.

Ben smiled, "In that case. I think I know what we have to do. But, we're going to have to jack another vehicle. And this one might be a little more risky than the usual pick up on the street."

The convention center stood out in the neighborhood, dominating the better part of a city block. The streets was a flurry of activity, traffic came and went, and a swarm of police vehicles, motorcycles, cruisers, vans, and patrol cars congested the entrances to the parking lot and just about anywhere one looked. The valets sat around looking bored and hungry for tips, but despite all the action none of them were working.

"So, this is obviously the place. Now what?" Diego looked at Ben, and then to Alastair who shrugged his shoulders.

Ben stepped in. "Right now, we just have to figure out the best way in, which I'm guessing would be that entrance to the parking lot. From there we'll have to find the press entrance, probably down a hallway in the back." He sounded confident that he knew what he was doing. As if he'd done this before.

"And you think they'll let us prance right in, huh?" Alastair voiced what was on Diego's mind.

Ben laughed off the comment. "Of course they wouldn't. You're missing the main part of the plan."

Diego spit on the sidewalk. "You gonna fill us in on that, or what? I've never seen so much heat at once.

This better be good, cuz I'm starting to think that you're full of shit."

Again, Ben laughed it off. "Sometimes you two are simple. No, were not just walking in there, obviously. Follow me, there's a better way."

He walked off down the sidewalk, away from the convention center. Even a block down, the streets were filled with law enforcement. As they walked Ben checked door handles on the cars they passed until he found one that was unlocked.

"Get in."

Diego looked at Ben in surprise. "You've got to be kidding me. Right here? Right now?"

Alastair stood behind Diego mirroring his expression.

"Right in front of them is usually the safest. None of those cops would ever think someone would be so brazen as to lift a car right before their eyes." He got in and started to break off the cover under the wheel.

Dubious, Alastair and Diego got into the passenger seat and the back. They both clicked on their seatbelts, trying to look like law abiding citizens. Ben lifted his head up as the car turned over and roared to life. He pulled out into traffic and started heading away from the convention center.

Alastair lit a cigarette and pulled the seat back, cracked the window slightly and looked over to Ben. "Now what? I thought we were heading into the convention."

"In this car? No way. No, we need better cover than this. That place is going to be filled with more cops than you or I have ever seen. We need a way to blend in, look like we belong there. And with the way you two look, that wouldn't happen in a million years. No, we're heading to pick something up."

Driving at a steady pace Ben steered the car away from the city center and toward the highway. He got on for two exits and then pulled off again, heading into an area full of warehouses and industrial-looking businesses. Up ahead a broadcast tower loomed above a two-story building, with several news vans parked in front. He pulled the vehicle around the block and parked with a view of the vans in plain sight.

"This is it. Now we wait." He put the car in neutral and left it idling.

Recognition started to spread across Alastair's face. From the back Diego spoke up, "Wait for what? We're nowhere near the convention anymore."

Impatient, Ben responded, "See those news vans up there. Any minute now, one of them is going to pull out and head for the convention. The news is going to be all over this thing. And we're going to be the news. Get it."

Diego started to protest but Alastair shushed him. "Shut up. It's a good plan. Makes perfect sense, and it's the perfect cover."

Ben nodded without saying anything while Diego looked out the window in silence, obviously not real-izing the full extent of the plan. After a few minutes three people left the building and entered one of the vans. A moment later they pulled away from the curb and started heading toward the highway.

Slow and steady Ben put the car in drive and followed the news van. A block from the highway he sped up and overtook the van, yanking the wheel and pulling in front of the newscasters, blocking their way.

"Now!" Leaving the car running, Ben jumped out and headed to the van.

Alastair and Diego did the same. Ben ran to the driver's side, opened the door, and yanked the driver out onto the street. Alastair motioned for Diego to go around back while he followed Ben's lead with the person in the passenger seat. In less than a minute they had expelled all of the news people and were backing the van up to get around the car blocking its way, speeding toward the highway while the three news people were left shouting in confusion.

"This is crazy, they'll be onto us right away!" Yelled Diego from the back of the van.

Ben kept his eyes on the road while responding, "This van was heading to the convention to cover the story. They'll never expect us to do the same. Carjackers wouldn't purposefully go to the biggest cop party in town. They'll be looking elsewhere, after they recover from the shock."

Recognition spread across Alastair's face. "Diego, take a look at that broadcasting equipment. See what you can figure out, we're going to need it. Slapjack, you're a genius. We can televise the whole thing. Find their press passes, it's our way in."

With a smug look on his face Ben kept driving, grateful that he didn't have to explain everything. They'd be back at the convention within ten minutes. And he had already scoped out the press entrance. They'd be able to stroll right in, and the cops knew better than to mess with the press during such an important unveiling of a large-scale city plan.

They came barreling off the freeway and tore down the street toward the convention center. When they were only a few blocks away Ben brought it down a notch and started driving under the speed limit, blending in with traffic. The city center was still abuzz with police, but less so than before. Presumably many of the officers had funneled into the convention. None of them even looked the way of the news vans. It was a perfect disguise due to the fact that the press was bound to be there and would not really stick out anywhere in the city. Ben cut across a few lanes and pulled into the line heading into the parking garage. Most of the cars in line were patrol cars, mixed in with highway patrol cruisers.

Ben took the ticket from the machine and the bar raised to let them in. He leaned over his shoulder and addressed Diego directly, "Get that equipment ready. Alastair can carry the briefcase with the mic equipment, and you grab the shoulder mount camera. I'll get the rest."

Diego handed Alastair the briefcase and busied himself with the rest of the gear. Ben pulled into a parking space and tossed the ticket onto the floor. They wouldn't be needing the van after this, and it would have certainly been called in by the time they were done. From the dash he snatched the clip-on press passes and divvied them out to the guys.

"These are our golden ticket. Nobody will question us with these pinned to our shirts." Ben pinned his to his collar while the other guys fussed with theirs.

"Golden ticket for the Golden Goose." Diego couldn't help himself, but Ben and Alastair just rolled their eyes.

They poured out of the van and Ben locked it on their way out, making sure to look like they were supposed to be there. No one paid them any mind as they made their way to the service elevator in the back of the parking lot. Once inside they were cramped in with banquet staff manning rolling cases filled with food prepped for one of the many events. The waiters didn't bat an eye at three pressmen riding the elevator. Their cover was working.

The elevator doors opened up to a long blank hallway, the interior of the building behind the facades put up for guests.

As the elevator door was closing Ben asked the guys inside, "Which way to the Cops of the Future convention?"

One of the guys pointed down the hall and motioned to take a right at the end. So far so good. They hoisted the film gear and made their way down the hall. Finding the door, Ben propped it open so that Alastair and Diego could make it through with the equipment. On the other side of the door the room was bustling with activity. Cops were everywhere and banquet staff ran to and fro setting up tables and chairs, while a whine from the PA system announced that it was being tested. They had arrived on time.

"Let's go check the schedule, so we can make sure that we're setting up in the right room." Ben really had this all figured out and the two followed him without question.

Alastair had never seen so many law enforcement officers in one place. The building was congested with sheriffs, regular police, plainclothes detectives, and Highway Patrol. The latter were easy to spot because most of them were Billys. Many of the officers seemed to be avoiding the Billys and one could almost cut a clear path between the clones and others. One side of the room was thick with Billys, the other not, and the tension dividing the room was palpable. Trying to blend in as best they could, they made their way to the information desk to find out which banquet hall that the conference would take place in, and to see what time Dale Thompson would be taking the lectern. It was distracting, to say the least, so many hotties in uniform. The tension in the air only made it more exciting.

They found a placard with the info they were looking for and noted where press was to set up. Most of the cops and Billys paid no attention to them, but a few eyed them suspiciously, as if their faces were familiar but they couldn't quite place them. With the Billys it was impossible to tell one from another, so there was no way of knowing if they had encountered any of them before, but it also could have just been the old cop stink eye. The three of them ignored any possible confrontation and made their way to the press corner and started setting up the equipment, trying to look like they knew what they were doing. A few of the other press guys looked them up and down. It gave Alastair the impression that most of the news people knew each other and their appearance had set off warning bells in some of the newscasters. He adjusted to make sure that his press badge was visible.

Diego had the camera up on a tripod and Alastair had pulled out the mic and managed to figure out how to set it up. Ben fiddled with knobs and somehow knew how to get the broadcast up and running.

"We're ready to roll guys. Just let me know whenever you want to go live." Ben seemed unconcerned that the news station might figure out what was going on. "We're sure to give them a real show."

Around the room the cops started to settle in. There was a clear divide across the room, all of the Billys on the right, and the other cops on the left, refusing to mingle. So, the contention on the force wasn't just a phenomenon in California. The Billys were unpopular here too, even though they had been delegated to the highways. Alastair imagined that many of the cops were there to try and protect their jobs.

Once all of the officers were seated a man went up to the podium and tapped the mic to make sure it was working. A stab of feedback shot through the loud-speakers before he introduced himself.

"Greetings everybody. Welcome to the Cops of the Future symposium. We're glad that you're here to learn about the next wave of law enforcement technology." There was a wave of sighs from the section where the regular cops were seated. The Billys sat in silence. The speaker continued, "I know that everyone has a lot of questions about where the program is going, and we're going to get to them all. There will be an extensive Q&A at the end of the seminar, and everyone will have the opportunity to voice their opinions. But first we have a few speakers lined up for you. Please give them the attention they deserve, and we should have plenty of time to cover everything. Now please give a warm welcome to Dale Thompson, a face I'm sure most of you will recognize."

A lackluster round of applause barely filled the room as a man made his way up to the stage.

"Holy shit. That's him." Diego spoke too loudly, and Alastair socked him on the arm to shut him up.

Dale Thompson shook hands with the presenter and took the lectern, looking around the room and making eye contact with as many of the officers as possible. There must have been over four hundred cops filling the room.

"Thank you for having me today. I know that many of you have trepidations about the Cops of the Future program, and believe me, I understand your concerns. Perhaps some of you don't know this, but I spent over thirty years on the force. I was chosen as a template for my track record, one that I am proud of; I suspect that many of you have similar, exemplary records."

He paused for effect and gazed at the crowd trying to discern who the "good cops" were. This gesture didn't go unnoticed and some of the cops fidgeted in their seats, betraying their discomfort.

"Some of you may have heard about the problems in California, and I'm here to explain what went wrong and how we can prevent those types of issues from occurring again." Several men in the audience made audible noises of protest. "Yeah, I know. Things went poorly there. And I know that working together we can create a force to be reckoned with, one that is corruption and scandal free."

For a moment he fiddled with a power point remote, unsure how to get it to work, before an AV tech approached and showed him how to click it on. The screen behind him lit up with charts full of crime rate statistics. The sound of the crowd suggested that they were already growing impatient.

Alastair whispered to Ben that they should probably get the broadcast started. The room felt like something was about to happen, and he didn't want to miss it. Also, the press guys around them would start to get suspicious if they weren't actually filming anything. Ben flipped the switches and got the gear rolling while Alastair held up the mic as he had seen reporters do, trying to look official.

Officers Jernigan and Troy walked into the room, arriving several minutes late, and were looking around for open seats when Troy noticed the corner where the press was set up.

"Those guys look familiar to you?" He spoke at regular volume even though the conference was in full swing. He didn't care what the speakers had to say, they had been ordered to attend.

Jernigan followed Troy's pointing finger to where the cameras were set up. For a moment all he saw was the news gear and the usual press entourage. Then recognition spread across his face.

"Are those the guys from the other day? From the chase?" He spoke more quietly than his partner.

Troy nodded and continued to stare at them from across the room, forgetting all about the search for a place to sit. Several of the cops he was standing in front of started grumbling for them to sit down. There were open seats near where the Billys sat, but they weren't about to align themselves with that side.

On stage Dale continued to go over the virtues of the Cops of the Future program, and as he spoke more and more hands went up for questions.

"Gentlemen, I appreciate the enthusiasm, but we'll reserve the Q&A until the end of the presentation."

A wave of grumbles rippled through the audience as their impatience grew. All of them had heard the propaganda and didn't need a patronizing repeat of what they had already been told. One of the guys behind Troy and Jernigan ran out of patience and stood up.

"Sit down or get of the way." He continued to stand, waiting for them to make a move.

Jernigan turned to face him, "Or what? You gonna make us? We're not taking orders from you, pick on your own department."

The face of the man complaining turned beet red and he took a step forward. Jernigan did the same and Troy stepped in further, crowding the guy making the complaint. Several of the sitting cops also stood up, sensing that some shit was about to go down. Noticing this, Jernigan's shoulders tightened and he moved into a fighting posture. Troy did the same.

"Sit down or get out."

That was the last straw. Jernigan threw a blow at the cop who had first stood up, decking him right on the jaw. Troy took a shot at the guy standing next to him, starting a ball rolling that could not be stopped. Seeing the commotion, Alastair tugged on Ben's arm and motioned for him to turn the camera on the action. Several seats were overturned as more and more officers were sucked into the brawl, and fights were breaking out all over the room. Many of the cops had taken the cue to express their frustration with the Billys, and the fighting began to concentrate itself on that side of the room.

From the stage Dale started pleading with them to stop the madness. "Hey, hey, we're all on the same side here. If it's that big of a deal we can take your questions now."

But his words were lost to the commotion. There was only one thing on everyone's minds now. Fists flew wildly as fight after fight broke out. The regular cops and the Billys were evenly numbered and the line between them was becoming a war zone. Ben swung the camera to and fro trying to catch everything that was happening, but it was getting too widespread and happening too fast to get it all in one frame. Next to them the other reporters were relaying the scene into their microphones frantically. Alastair, having no need to do the same, took his opening and started running up the aisle to where a shocked Dale Thompson stood looking at the scene of the riot. The cops all but ignored him, having turned their attention to the Billys, who were putting up the fight of their lives. Alastair had never seen so many of them in one place, and watching them fighting together made him want a piece all that more.

The chaos was centered where the fight had broken out. Jernigan and Troy were taking on several men each, throwing punches with abandon, and receiving blows themselves. A nasty right came out of nowhere and landed squarely on Jernigan's face, forcing him to stumble and fall into Troy's arms.

For a moment all stood still as they looked at each other. The fight forgotten and time slowing down. Troy leaned down and as he righted Jernigan and they came face to face, he planted a kiss directly onto his waiting lips. Somehow in their embrace a circle had parted around them, leaving them free from the violence. And out of nowhere the brawl started to settle down. They stopped kissing for a moment and looked around to see what the change had been. All around them Billys and beat cops were starting to embrace. Where once blows had been exchanged, now many of them were kissing deeply, and some were starting to shed their uniforms.

As Alastair moved toward the stage, where an astonished Dale was still standing motionless, he looked at the scene in amazement. It was a wet dream come true. Uniforms, one by one, fell to the floor. The sound of what was happening was not unlike the riot, but now it rippled with waves of pleasure rather than anger. Everything that had the force all pent up was now unraveling into something much different. He wanted to jump into the center of it all and be swallowed up by them like a ball pit. And surely he would have, if not for the fact that the Golden Goose was standing right there in front of him. It was now or never.

He turned to look over his shoulder and Ben and Diego both gave him the thumbs up. Ben was panning the camera around to get it all but then handed it to Diego before diving in to join the action. Alastair pointed at Diego and then up to Dale on the stage, sending the message that he had to film what was about to happen next. Sure that his point had gotten across, he resumed heading through the orgy up to the stage.

He mounted the stage where Dale still stood next to the podium with a look of astonishment all over his rugged face. The Golden Goose was no doubt the source of the DNA for all of the immaculate Billys, but he had that quality of originality, the look of experience, and the cocksuredness that could only come with age. Still, he stood frozen not knowing what to do with himself.

Alastair joined him at the lectern. From the stage the scene unfolding in front of them was a masterpiece of hedonism. Billys and regular cops were fucking. Billys and Billys were fucking. All the violence had melted away into sex. Hot sex. All the moans of pleasure morphed together into one chorus of fuck sounds. All the departments of the force were now one in their pleasure. And the news was broadcasting all of it.

Dale was leaning up against the lectern, sweating profusely and rocking back and forth. Alastair came up behind him and wrapped his arms around his body, finding the buckle of his belt and loosening it enough to get his pants to drop. Dale didn't even fight it; he was too consumed with watching everything that was happening in front of him. Alastair freed himself from his pants, and not believing that it was finally happening, he entered Dale right there in front of the entire force. As he plunged deep into Dale, he heard the ex-cop's pleasure sounds amplified through the PA system. Dale's face was pressed up right against the mic, and every moan that came from deep within him echoed through the convention hall at top volume.

As he thrust himself in and out of Dale, holding onto him by the shoulders, he spared a glance over to Diego, who was pointing the camera directly at them. He looked around for Ben, but he was lost in the crowd, no doubt taking or giving with one cop after another. Alastair would have liked to fuck them all, but Dale bent over the lectern was pulling him in like a mesmerized animal. He continued to pound away at him, bringing himself close to climax and then slowing down trying to prolong the moment. When he couldn't stand it anymore, he took a step back, holding the base of his cock, took a step to the edge of the stage, then shot his load into the crowd of fucking cops. It landed on faces, hands, asses, and everywhere in between. It was the hardest cum of his life.

Breathless, Dale still stood at the lectern, his dick quivering and ready to direct him like a compass. He followed its lead and leapt into the crowd, giving in to the flesh from every angle possible. On stage, Alastair smiled with satisfaction, zipped himself up, took one last look at Diego waving the camera around, catching it all, and ran to the emergency exit on the side of the room.

Back at the seedy motel, Alastair could hardly believe what had just happened. Their infiltration of the convention had gone beyond his wildest dreams. He had no idea where Slapjack and Diego had gone, but no doubt they were lost in the throes of what had just happened, or maybe still at it. Every time he thought of the Golden Goose his heart raced. He had screwed the ultimate Billy; he would be the envy of every guy in the unofficial Billy Club.

As he sat on the edge of the bed, fully nude, he flipped on the television and found a news channel. Much of what was being shown was censored out with black bars that nearly filled the screen. But despite the censorship it was no stretch of the imagination what was going on. Some of the footage must have been taken from the other news people, but some of it was clearly from the camera that Diego had been manning. He saw the footage pan over to the stage and he watched as the black bar that covered him and Dale suggested what was happening behind it. Below the footage a ticker bar ran the details as a newscaster talked about the scandal that was now overtaking the force and the demise of the Cops of the Future program in the city, and possibly across the nation.

Just thinking about it made his dick hard.

A GLOBE, GRANITE UNDERFOOT

BY J. W. STEED

"For my part, I travel not to go anywhere, but to go. I travel for travel's sake. The great affair is to move; to feel the needs and hitches of our life more nearly; to come down off this feather-bed of civilization, and find the globe granite underfoot and strewn with cutting flints."

— Robert Louis Stevenson,

Travels with a Donkey in the Cévennes

DAY FIVE

"Reverend Father. Wait." As we near the crest of the Great Road, I dare touch Prior Amodeo upon the shoulder. We haven't surveyed for dangers in our haste to escape the cypress forest's lengthy shadows. "Just for a moment, if you please."

Without a question, the older man takes a knee. His hand searches for the arc blade at his side. "As you say, Brother."

I hunch down beside him, huddling close as I dare. Toward a relentless horizon stretches the Great Road, perhaps the most ancient ruin remaining of the long-vanished race we know as the Salix. Countless blocks of rough limestone interlock together underfoot in a span thirty meters wide, some carved, many broken, all thousands upon thousands of years old. Toward the planet's unforgiving horizon, the avenue stretches, bounded upon either side by endless groves of what the Brotherhood's taxonomist termed *cupressus concavus*.

That poor man. Six weeks the taxonomist had sojourned through space to this distant planet known as Plum, only to alight from our vessel and classify a single tree before stumbling into a nest of lethal grubs. An ignominious end, and only the first in a sequence of missteps and tragedies. Most of the Brothers had quickly insisted that ours was a cursed expedition.

Spotting something, I point down the sloping road. A pack of the oversized creatures writhe upon the pavement before one of the dark, square, plinth-like roadside platforms erected every few kilometers. These creatures are not like the grubs I used to overturn while spading dirt in the Carolinas; they are longer and thicker than a grown man's body. Soft and pulsating beneath their grossly white skin. Like cooked bacon fat, they glisten in Plum's perpetual golden hour. Clusters of them convulse and thrash in puddles of the previous night's rain at a distance below.

The prior puts his arm around my shoulders and murmurs into my ear. "We shall go around."

His very proximity makes me shiver. I harbor thoughts for Prior Amodeo I should not. Thoughts unbefitting an initiate for his superior. Yet my carnal yearnings are unsuited for this time and this place, when our priority should be wending a safe trail. Thus, I nod and allow him to take the lead.

So aged is this section of the Great Road that its central section has sunk into the earth below. During Plum's nightly rainstorms, floods of water cascade through these channels in the road's most inclined sections, forming torrents strong enough to sweep a man away and batter him upon dislodged pavement—as we discovered our second night. The Prior is vigorous, though. Muscular, beneath his tunic and trousers. Forty-four years, to my twenty-four. Upon block after block, his boots nimbly land as he positions himself mid-road. I scout around him for unseen hazards.

When, from his perch, he points at a grapefruit-sized rock at my feet and gestures I should hand it to him, I obey. Like an athlete, he pauses for a moment, judging his aim. His tunic rises when he throws, exposing a strip of fur and firm flesh that, with danger so near, should not arouse me as much as it does. The rock arcs over the nearest collective of grubs and bounces off the plinth's base and into the cypresses; I watch as the grubs roil and wriggle in its direction. "Another," Amodeo demands. Again, he launches the stone up and away.

I do not stand idly by. Yesterday I had fashioned a slingshot of sorts by whittling down a Y-shaped cypress branch, then adding a strip of synthetic leather and the elastic ties from my satchel. With it, I lob rocks of my own, herding the grubs off the road. We both sigh with relief as the first cluster vanishes into the ashy roadside loam and burrows underground.

In their wake, other clusters follow. Their progress isn't quick, by any means, but within a few minutes, the Great Road is clear enough for us to continue our journey west. We work well together, the Prior and I. "Do they hear, then?" I feel compelled to ask.

Amodeo considers. "They have no visible appendages. Perhaps they sense vibrations from a distance."

"How distant, do you think?"

The prior hefts his pack while considering my question with gravity. "It is not a hypothesis I wish to test. Nor you, I suspect. Come, Brother Sorrowful." With a look behind us, he once more places his hand on my back. Despite the hardships we have endured since we became stranded from the rest of our expedition team, I am always alert for these little physical attentions he bestows upon me; I focus more upon the square where his palm warms my spine than any dangers that lie ahead. "Let us proceed."

There is little use in asking where. I know already what his reply will be. "Down the Great Road?"

Beneath Plum's blood orange sun, he picks a path among the uneven blocks, his unpowered arc blade in one strong hand. "Yes. Down the Great Road, with cheer in our hearts. Have faith, Sorrowful," he chides, not ungently. "You and I may be stranded together here, for now. But the Brotherhood does not abandon its own. When they locate us, they will come. Besides." He gestures at the expanse of carved rubble that stretches without visible end to as far as the eye can see. "All roads have a source and a destination, with byways in between. While we wait for rescue, we may as well make ourselves of use and see what we can find along the way."

Counterarguments accumulate upon my tongue. If the Brotherhood does not abandon its own, why had the rest of our expedition fled our landing site, marooning only the Prior and me upon this accursed planet? But I swallow those doubts and follow. Not only because he is my superior, but because I have promised myself I shall protect him.

Neither of us fully comprehends the dangers of Plum. I refuse to allow the Prior to become its next victim.

DAY SEVEN

Water courses down Amodeo's naked body. His heavy pectorals channel a stream down his sternum, where it flows over his sturdy trunk to blossom at his thick cock's root. A runnel arches and spatters from that meaty, uncut protrusion, finally splashing onto the forest's mossy floor. I shouldn't look, but I can't tear my eyes away.

The man is beautiful to behold. Four and a half decades have not diminished the strength of his torso, nor the sheer lumber-like heft of his thighs. The auburn curls atop his head, through which gray threads wend, frame a face that for me defines masculinity: a snubbed nose, a lightly bearded jaw, a blunt, square chin. He is the father I wish I had—though my feelings for him are decidedly unfilial. Also, unlike my own daddy, Amodeo's eyes are always kind whenever he looks upon me.

He does so now, laughing at my shyness. "One more dousing, Brother Sorrowful. If you please."

Oh, how I wish to please. I have yearned for the Prior since the moment he helped me aboard the *Beagle*. I'd been a late addition to the spacecraft's manifest, dispatched with great speed from the Brotherhood's largest chapterhouse in the Free Scotias; my connecting shuttle had arrived upon the moon of Deimos with less than an hour to spare before the expedition's departure. By myself, hauling all my own bags, I'd had to navigate my way across the United Settlements jump station to find our departure point.

My formal Scholastic leathers, in their unblemished blinding white of a brand-new initiate, attracted everyone's scrutiny. Full U.S. citizens and indentureds alike stared in my wake. When I'd arrived at the *Beagle's* berth, panting and exhausted, shoulder aching from my duffels, I was certain that the vessel would have departed without me. The Scholastic Brotherhood already has a public reputation—deserved, in truth—of welcoming malcontents and of conscripting the irredeemable. If I'd found myself stranded upon Deimos, I would not have enjoyed surviving two weeks of suspicion and hostility before a Brotherhood shuttle could be sent to collect me.

Upon the jump craft's lowered drop deck stood a strapping older man in his monastic gray leathers. He inspected a data pad. Supply crates surrounded him; a last-minute delivery of Heal-Me biologics bearing the logo of a Pharmafarm. Wavy curls of dark auburn hung to his shoulders, and his tunic lay open across the chest to his waist to display a toned musculature. A bright red sash cinched his waist; he'd stuffed his wide-legged breeches into calf-high black boots. To my dazzled eyes, he looked like a pirate of a distant age: all he lacked was the eyepatch.

"Brother Sorrowful!" the man had called, unsurprised to see me. How did he know my name? Of course: I was the boy in initiate's whites. Perhaps he mistook as intimidation how agog I was at the sight of him, a reassuring masculine presence amidst United Settlements chaos. He stuck out a big, rough hand to haul me onto the platform, then surveyed me once I'd clambered aboard. "Did they not feed you lads at the chapterhouse?"

"I..."

"What do you think of our vessel, Sorrowful?"

His was not a rhetorical question. I was unused to being asked for my opinion, especially by a fine-looking stranger who surely had lived an entire life before I was even conceived. My overawed mouth worked without thinking. "She seems a well-built craft, Brother."

"Reverend Father," he corrected. Before a flush could completely overtake my face, though, he added with reassurance, "But the fault is mine for not introducing myself. I am Prior Amodeo. I lead the cultural branch of the expedition." I stammered something apologetic, but he heard not. Instead, he asked, "Are you ready for an adventure, Sorrowful?"

Determined not to embarrass myself, I'd nodded with vigor. "Yes, Reverend Father. I am."

"Then welcome aboard." The deck lifted from the platform, swallowing us both into *The Beagle's* interior.

In that moment, I knew I would follow Prior Amodeo anywhere.

"Sorrowful?" His query recalls me to the present, where he stands only an arm's length away, naked.

"I apologize, Reverend Father." The cypresses of this planet are not like those of home; their sturdy, broad leaves curve at their base into shapes like pitchers that capture rainwater by the liter. They collect it so effectively that very little falls to the ground below, nights. Our taxonomist had spied the shaggy tendrils of what I call fen bladders floating between the trees and, confusing them for Spanish moss, had deemed the forest trees cypresses.

The balloon-like bladders, however, are their own form of vegetable life. Moss-like filaments hang below their bloated bodies, which drift high above in colonies between the cupped cypress leaves. To remain afloat, the tips of those hanging coils synthesize hydrogen from the water the cypresses collect; up and down in clusters by the thousand they drift, an additional cover from the nightly rains that replenish the forests and make the Great Road so dangerous.

With the tip of Amodeo's long walking stick, I shove away a cluster of the bushy balloons and prod the bottom of one low-hanging cypress pitcher, tilting it groundward to release the warmed liquid within. Amodeo tilts back his head beneath the stream and runs his fingers through the russet locks, shaking his head and shoulders like an Irish Setter under the hose. A torrent of droplets gleam in Plum's eternal red sunset.

Once again, I avert my eyes, lest I stare too much. His laughter at being clean for the first time in so long, though, echoes throughout the grove, loud and clear. Even the gravest heart must lighten to that sound. My own does.

One week in total have we stood upon this planet and gazed upon its unvarying scenery. We have been stranded upon Plum since our third day: it was then that Prior Amadeo and I had set out on a two-man overnight trek to survey the road ahead, unaware the Tell-Me he wore upon his tunic had only enough power for a few hours.

On day four, we returned to find remnants of chaos at the expedition's encampment. Mud strewn everywhere. Supplies overturned. Bunks abandoned and left topsy-turvy as if something had aroused the Brothers in the midst of their sleep. Most ominous of all, tracks of blood. Broken branches and disturbed ground told me something large had dragged one of our own, injured or worse, toward the Great Road.

Our only ship-to-ground shuttle was gone, leaving behind compacted earth and scorch marks where its landing gear had rested. The Prior and I had been forsaken: the only two humans upon Plum.

Not once since has either of us felt like laughing. His elation infects me now, though—enough that I mischievously tip the receptacle of rainwater squarely upon the Prior's head, leaving him drenched.

For a moment, we stand still and stare at the other. Diamond beads glisten upon his shoulders, his chest hair, his pubes. He seems pleased that I've forgotten to fret. "But you must bathe, too," he jokes, then shakes his mane to soak me.

The Prior brooks none of my objections, instead taking from my clutch his walking stick and using it to shepherd away a formation of the floating bladders overhead. "Make haste, while the waters are still warm." Again, I protest. The only time I've been naked before Amodeo was—well, I cannot recall without mortification the night he caught me in an indiscretion, three weeks ago. "You cannot be thinking about our dinner," he says, sternly. "I know you've already foraged."

"I set aside plenty of sponge fruit and billiard nuts, yes."

Without shame for his nudity, the Prior puts his hands upon his lips and laughs long and loud once more. "You've called them billiard nuts?"

My hands work the air as I try to explain. "They're round and shiny, like billiard balls." Roasted, they taste something like pistachio. Pounded between rocks, their flour makes a passable hoecake. I meant the label of *sponge fruit* to be just as self-explanatory. Once gourds growing at the base of the forest floor have been relieved of their shells, what remains is a dense, airy edible, the texture of a slice of angel food.

"Oh, Sorrowful." The Prior spins me around and begins to untie my field tunic. "What an opportunity. We are as Adam and Eve, naked and assigning names to the fruit of the earth and the creatures of the field." He tugs the lightweight cloth over my head. I stumble back to unfasten my trousers on my own, before he can completely undress me like a child. He at least grants me a slight modesty while I do so, prodding experimentally at the cypress pitchers above to find one laden with water. "Your files indicated advanced survival skills. The chapterhouse sent you to Deimos after you impressed them by completing your solo postulant field assignment in record time."

"I grew up off the grid. A bunker rat," I explain, removing my boots and pants. "In the Carolina Sovereign States."

"Yes," is all he says. "A rough life?"

"Rough, but practical." Rebels, they called us. Illegals. I was the seventh son of a seventh son: any decent full-fledged United Settlements citizen would deem my family's size obscene—yet growing up, I knew of many larger. Moving between encampments and evading Enforcers often meant surviving in rough terrain for days or weeks on end. This Great Road expedition was my first; it feels good to be recognized for the wilderness skills I'd taken for granted. "When you're not sure where you'll spend the next night, you learn to live off the land."

"Still, I'm sure you've never had a shower like this." Without warning, he lets loose a torrent of water from above. I gasp at the shock of its temperature, which hovers at the point of being warm enough to cheer, yet still deliciously cool. Only after the initial dousing do I remember that Amodeo can see every inch of me. My hands scamper to cover my private parts. I hate to consider what he thinks of my body, so lanky next to his, boyish and short adjacent to his masculine bulk. We are a study in contrasts. The Prior only laughs, though, tipping the bucket-like leaf to release the rest of its contents. "Wash that dust off you, Sorrowful."

Enough dirt has penetrated my skin that the water first must form a layer of mud before I can rinse it clean. And the Prior is correct: I've bathed in streams and from stale pools in the bunkers below ground, but never had I enjoyed warmed rainwater on a red-sunned, twilight planet light years away from home. "This is crazy," I sputter, dancing beneath a second delivery of the stuff.

"And only you and I have the privilege of the experience!" Amodeo tosses me the chamois from my pack. It's no towel, but I've dried off with worse. "One day, when you are a very old man and I am decrepit beyond recognition..." His head turns when I snort. That could never happen. "We will reminisce of this adventure and laugh together."

I finish wiping the moisture from my skin and begin to shimmy back into my leggings. "Do you really think the *Beagle* is above, searching for us?"

"Yes, I believe it. No, I know." In that moment, as we resume our attire and regard each other from eyelashes fringed with droplets, I almost believe, too. "Besides, protocol demands they remain and search."

"But we have no working Tell-Me. No tracker."

"What is your name?" Without warning, he seizes my shoulder. His strong grip causes me to stutter. "Not your Brotherhood name. What were you called before?"

On my conscription, the chapterhouse had daily told me to forget my old name and life. Shedding those was a new start. A way to free myself of the shackles of the past. One day, I will choose a Brotherhood name of my own, but for now, I am known only as Sorrowful, assigned to me by the Registrar after one glance at my face.

Recalling to my lips my old given name feels like a betrayal, or a trap.

"You can say."

I'm still hesitant, but I decide to share. "Ayden."

"Ayden," he repeats, staring into my eyes. "We will be rescued. The Brothers remaining will be watching for a sign. And I promise you: a sign will be delivered them." Heretic I may be, but the pseudo-religious vocabulary of the Brotherhood often gnaws at my patience; its insistence on signs and belief tests credulity. We are stranded on this planet with no way to contact our brethren. We do not know if even the *Beagle* remains in orbit. I see no way home. "Do you trust me?"

My response is automatic. "Of course, Reverend Father." He is being strong for the both of us. That moves me enough to silence my fears.

"Ayden." The sound of my old name snaps me alert. "None of that Reverend Father business. Just Amodeo, from now on." He draws close to place one assuring hand on my shoulder. The other cups my chin, centering my face to his. "We will survive this ordeal, but we have to rely upon each other. Now. I ask once more. Do you trust me?"

We stand so near. Part of my imagination follows a great road of its own into territories it should not: I imagine what it would be like to have him press his lips against mine, to allow his hands to linger upon me and press against my hardness. How I wish this moment might never end.

"I do," I whisper.

"And I you." He lets loose my jaw and gives my shoulder a squeeze that infuses me with joy. Then, without warning, he pulls his damp chamois through his fist and whips it against my buttocks. When I cry out, more in surprise than from pain, he whoops and does it again. "We are on an adventure. Not a penance!"

I want to believe, like he does. For the moment, I'll allow him to shoulder the burden of conviction for the both of us.

We work in silence until nightfall. I've surrounded tonight's camp with a circle of the brambly brush that I've observed the grubs avoid. With my arc dagger on the burn setting, I light a small fire; I use the same blade on its lowest weapon power to slice open a sponge fruit. Amodeo nods as I hand him a portion. "I was aware of your general background, but not its extent. I thought perhaps Cellarer Avery had taught you how to find food in the field, on our voyage here."

I doubt he can see it, but disgrace flushes my face, burning hotter than any campfire. "No," I choke, unable to swallow. I don't like talking about Cellarer Avery.

Amodeo impales a chunk of the fruit upon a stick and holds it over the fire. A trick of the light catches his face in profile. For the first time, I notice a narrow, faded scar sluicing down his cheek. He prods a little further into the one topic I would rather avoid. "I would understand if you grieve his loss."

"No!" I say again, horrified at the idea. Avery, in charge of the expedition's provisions, had been one of the earliest casualties of this expedition. Storm floods after dark on the Great Road had swept him away. I doubted many grieved his passing. Myself, least of all. "Cellarer Avery was not...was not a good man." I turn my head, revisiting Avery's midnight grunts of gratification. Nightly had that vile man extracted pleasure from my pain. The recollection shames me.

"Wasn't he? How do you mean?" Something in my tone, or perhaps in the guarded way I spoke, rouses Amodeo's protective nature. He had been perched on half a chunk of granite tumbled from the road on the other side of the campfire. Swiftly and without warning, he sits upon the other half, next to me. "Ayden, if he interfered with you…if he hurt you in any way, you can…"

Remembering anything having to do with the Cellarer already sickens me to the core, but Amodeo's sudden concern makes me feel almost…well…*angry*. Where had he been on the *Beagle*, those late nights when that bastard Avery prowled the lower decks, trying to jab his slimy pecker into anything young and tight? Why the sympathy for the man's wrongdoings now, when he was a week dead and gone?

Our second night after planetfall, Cellarer Avery had dragged me by the ear outside into the storms, intent on frightening me into doing his bidding. He had been drunk past reckoning and ignored the other initiates who cowered in the brightly lit opening of our tent, pleading for him to leave me be, so intent was he upon forcing me outdoors into the danger of darkness. When I'd fought free, he'd chased me in the wrong direction and stumbled unawares into the deluge of water channeled down the road's sunken center.

Where had the Prior been that night?

"Don't," I say, contention electrifying the word.

That's when arises the very sound we have come to dread.

How can I describe what we have heard every nightfall on this planet? All of us in the expedition had chilled at its deafening reverberations, the very first evening we made camp. The phenomenon comes from the direction of the Great Road itself, no matter on which side one stands. Always it arrives after the sun has set and left the skies empurpled, but before the rains begin.

The first night, Brother Trucekeeper, another of the initiates, had shivered in his cot and said it resembled the crunch of human bones being slowly ground into dust. Another was reminded of the torturous scrape of claws across a giant chalkboard. Even the *Beagle's* spooked pilot, Brother Makepeace, who had been on more Brotherhood expeditions than any of us and had never heard the like, stood in the doorway of the mess tent, listened intently, and immediately advised we cut our losses and undertake the journey home. "The dirge of the judgement of ages," he'd shuddered.

In that cacophony of percussive strikes, screeches, and what had to be the friction of stone against stone, some were reminded of feral animals mating in the shadows, others of the din of rust-covered chains dragged down a dungeon corridor. Brother Swiftdare, perhaps the only initiate I called friend, whispered to me that it sounded like the opening of a graveyard vault from within, as the restless dead pushed aside the heavy stone.

To me, though, the nightly cacophony brought to mind a sound I used to dread more than any other: those frantic moments back in the Carolina Sovereign States when we would pack an underground bunker, the dozens of our own family and often the many more of other clans as well, to evade patrolling Enforcers. Into one of hundreds of airless tombs we would descend with nothing more than candles for light and sometimes not even those, to stare overhead through the hatch at one last rectangle of sky.

With a scrape and a clamor, someone would slam shut the bulkhead doors. Then would follow a *sshh-sshh-sshh* and the rasping of wood against metal, as a scout outside would surround and cover the entrance with brush and rubble. Under the earth, in the dark, I would shiver and suffocate, not knowing when next I might breathe freely again.

That is what I remember, night after night on this planet, when the Great Road begins to groan. United Settlements orbital surveys had declared Plum a planet free of fauna. Yet the grubs exist. And something even more terrible is out there, making these bone-chilling noises.

Whatever exasperation I feel at Amodeo instantly evaporates. "Hold still," he whispers into my ear. The advice is unnecessary. Already, my breathing is shallow. My pulse quickens apace.

Tonight, the discord is nearer than ever, seemingly just over the ridge of ashy loam running beside the Great Road. I'm conscious of Amodeo's arm creeping around my shoulder and drawing me close. Close enough that I can feel the thud of his own heart through my own rib cage.

The volume intensifies, causing us both to shiver. He looks around, then spies his arc blade next to his bedroll, on the fire's other side. It lies too far out of his reach, but I am close enough to lean forward and retrieve it. He accepts it with a nod, flips off the safety, and squeezes the hilt. I hear the weapon power up with a single ascending electronic scale. The arc completes its circuit and blazes into light.

I withdraw the arc dagger from its scabbard at my hip and hold it at the ready. As an afterthought, I withdraw my slingshot as well. He nods in approval and huddles close.

The memory of that muddy, bloody trail left in our abandoned landing site haunts me. If a score of remaining Brothers had been attacked and terrorized into leaving Plum's atmosphere, what chance did we two have against the same foes? But then I hear the patter of a raindrop high above upon the canopy of cypress branches and fen bladders, followed by another. Then a dozen more. The sprinkle becomes a shower, the shower a downpour.

And the terrible sounds recede into the night, as they always do.

The pair of us remain in our posture for a moment. Then the Prior shuts off the arc blade to the accompaniment of a downward musical flourish. I maintain my grip on both my dagger and my slingshot. "Get some sleep, Rev...Amodeo," I tell him, every nerve ajangle. "I'll keep first watch."

He nods, the bravado from our afternoon showers vanished. With the gait of a rattled man, he rises and pulls his bedroll next to mine, then positions his blade nearby. "I think it best we hew close, henceforth," he murmurs before he settles close.

I find myself in full agreement. Beneath the canopy of bladders shifting gently among the tree branches, sheltering us from the bulk of the storm, he curls upon his side and closes his eyes. With pleasure, I watch the man curl into himself. "Ayden?"

I startle guiltily. Perhaps he knows my eyes have been upon him. "Yes?"

"Thank you for sharing your name. I am glad you are with me." His voice is already sleepy, like a little boy's.

A simple declaration of affection. I wish I had the courage to return it. What I can do, however, is to watch over him for the next few hours. Weapons in my clutch, I sit on guard, alert to the night's dangers.

FOURTEEN DAYS
BEFORE PLANETFALL

Were it not for a twist of fate, I would not have joined the Scholastic Brotherhood at all.

I had only just turned nineteen when the Carolinas underwent the great scouring—two weeks of assault when masses of Enforcers descended to squash the Sovereign States movement for good. Years it had taken, but the inter-system government had acquired the location of every hideout, every underground bunker, every nest among the cities' rubble. With so many Enforcers suddenly everywhere at once, the rebels had nowhere to run. We were all scooped up and transported to United Settlements Employment Reassignment facilities. My daddy had a different name for those government institutions: prisons.

Illegals, we were branded. A scourge. Non-citizens. Not long before, much of the civilized systems and their worlds had only just emerged from the two years of the second great pandemic. The Sovereign States had largely been spared. It seemed mighty convenient, my daddy pointed out, for United Settlements suddenly to produce tens of thousands of healthy menial laborers to replace some of the deceased. Even more convenient that since we all were deemed criminals, corporations wouldn't have to pay their new workforce.

For months, I sat in my cell and watched as officers sentenced all the people I knew in the world to every corner of the galaxy. Of my six brothers, four were assigned to munitions manufacturing plants in different systems; the two eldest were condemned for life with my daddy to hard toil on a low-atmosphere planet, for their part in the Greensboro bombings. The womenfolk tended to receive gentler assignments. My one sister and her younglings were transported to a farm world to tend sheep, which sounded mighty nice.

One by one, I watched my kin sold off to the highest bidders. Every familiar face disappeared without a farewell, never to be seen again. Not much love was lost as I watched them go. I know I sound heartless, but children in the Sovereign States were taught to cherish so-called liberty over family. Carolinas families splintered constantly. Mamas disappeared; daddies got shot or blown up. Liberty, though, was supposed to live forever.

Besides, I was only ever an afterthought to my clan. Overlooked. Another mouth to feed. All my life, I'd been a bit player in their more important stories. Can a pawn upon the chessboard truly love its king and queen, when it knows it's merely one of many, there for the winnowing?

Nearly a year I waited in a cell before it was my turn to be disposed of. Two weary Reassignment officers regarded my slumped figure from behind the console of a one-way Show-Me. I could see through the back of the transparent display in front of them and was conscious that they were reading my files upon its surface, but to me, nothing was visible. "Name: Ayden Laclos. Age: twenty," read the more bored of the officers.

He read aloud a list of my alleged offenses, none of which I'd accomplished on my own, exactly, but formed a catalog of what I was—a third-generation surplus illegal with no birth certificate or residency license, an able-bodied individual with none of the standardized mandated work credits, the child of criminals wanted in connection with...etcetera, etcetera. I'd no choice in any of those things, so I sat still and sullen to await my verdict.

"Arcturus Prime. Cobalt mines," decreed the officer, without so much as a glance my way. I froze. I'd hoped for a farming world, like my sister. The mines were a death sentence. Everyone knew it.

"Come on, Alph." The second officer at least took the time to regard me through the Show-Me's glossy display. "Look at the kid."

True, I was malnourished then, and preternaturally pale. No one had cut my dark hair in months. Lanks of it fell long and shaggy over my face. "What about him?" said the first officer.

"He won't last ten fucking minutes in those mines, that's what."

"He's almost of age."

"Almost. Not yet." The milder of the officers indicated a portion of the display off to the side. "Look. The Scholastic Brotherhood is always desperate for recruits."

"'Cause they're kooks. Can this little shit even read?"

"I can read," I said, perking up a little. We had books in the bunkers—real books, not the AI slop force-fed citizens through their machines. I'd buried my nose in their pages whenever I could. The old Greek and Roman mythologies were what I loved the most. Tales of Janus of the two faces. Dionysus, the reveler. Prometheus, bringer of fire. Anything involving books sounded better than manual labor.

"You know anything about the Brotherhood, kid?" I shook my head at the nicer officer. "They're oddballs. Pretend monks, like on the Show-Me historical programs. Not religious, though. They study old civilizations, alien sites, that kind of stuff. You might like them."

"Kooks, chasing monsters." The first officer rapped on the display to get my attention. "What's your flavor, bunker rat? Mines, or monsters?"

The decision wasn't difficult. Yet until we landed upon the planet of Plum, the only monster I'd encountered among the Brothers was Cellarer Avery on the *Beagle*. Although thinking of him makes me recoil, Avery wasn't a terrible-looking man. His only unattractive features were small, suspicious eyes that constantly darted to and fro as he spoke, sunk deep in an otherwise ordinary face, and a complexion so pale it looked almost transparent.

Other Brothers seemed to regard him well enough. As he slung meals onto aluminum trays, he would greet every man by name. He attended briefings when he could, though his duties didn't require his presence. His primary responsibilities were keeping everyone fed and maintaining the ship's water recirculation system. A team player, I'd heard one of the senior Brothers call him.

But oh, after lights-out, once he'd knocked back a drink or two, he'd transform. I'd known Averys among the bunker folk. Mostly married men with silent inclinations for tender youths of twenty-one or twenty-two—boys old enough to be plied with pretty words and corn liquor or illicit tobacco, in out of the way spaces where nobody might see. Word would get around sooner or later about these shifty figures, but the Carolina States folk were clannish enough that a predator could get away with anything short of maiming his prey before anyone would step in.

Word had gotten around about Cellarer Avery, too, at least down in the lowest deck where we initiates bunked. Our cabins there were only semi-private, with no hatch covers, all opening into a common area. When the Cellarer would make his way from room to small room, supposedly to say goodnight to the new recruits, we all could hear his oily progress. During the first weeks of the sojourn from Deimos, he'd appear to proffer us shortbreads from the kitchen or candies from his private stash. Recognizing his type, I feigned sleep.

United Settlements brats, though, are all raised staring at their Show-Mes, grabbing every meal hot from a Cook-Me, somehow arriving at their mid-twenties without a callus or a trace of dirt on their hands. Much as I grew up envying that kind of life, it meant my fellow initiates were soft. Childlike, even. Brother Swiftdare—pretty blue-eyed Brother Swiftdare with the curly blond locks and the blushing cheeks—was a year older than I. Yet he had no idea how to handle a pest like Avery. He first made the mistake of accepting the older man's little confections. Then, a few nights later, he allowed Avery to cajole him into taking a nip from his flask. Later still, when the Cellarer began taking liberties with his hands, I started hearing little yips and cries of alarm from Swiftdare's bunk.

Then, one night two weeks before our scheduled arrival upon Plum, I heard a muffled lamentation, shortly after Avery slithered into Swiftdare's cabin at last to collect his debt. "No. No. *No*...!"

Unlike the other initiates, I didn't intend to lie in my own bed and pretend I didn't overhear Swiftdare's deflowering. Clad only in the nightshirt issued to initiates, I sprang from my bunk and flew across the common room to his chamber. "Brother Swiftdare," I said as loudly as possible so that everyone could hear. "If you cry out because your stomach ails you, I've soothing peppermints in my nightstand." I jerked my head, indicating he should go.

He hesitated for a moment, then finally realized the escape I offered. "Thank you, Brother Sorrowful," he sniffed, pale and shaken from his near violation.

I waited until his footsteps receded before continuing, with as much volume as before. "Cellarer Avery, the Prior wishes to speak with you."

"The Prior?" Avery was taken aback at my invocation of his superior. He did not think to question why the Prior would have enlisted, of all folk, a barefoot initiate in his nightshirt as an emissary.

"Yes. Please, if you'll accompany me."

I led the way from the initiates' quarters into the lowermost section of the *Beagle* reserved for the sewage systems and general storage, through one of the accordion-pleated sliding hatches, and up the narrow stairwell beyond. Only then, well out of earshot, did I wheel on him.

"Leave Swiftdare alone."

Avery blinked, then colored. "Did the Prior...?" He realized my deceit and became angry. "Has the boy complained to anyone? Someone important?"

"No, but he will if you push him too far."

"Oh, will he, now?" His lack of remorse was palpable. "Who are you to give me orders? What would the Prior say? Whose story will he believe?" On the turn of a dime, he began to wheedle, softly imploring, "There's no harm done. I barely touched the lad." Then, suspicious once more, "Sweet on him yourself, are you then?"

I already knew that should this matter be taken to any of the superiors, Avery's word would win against ours. That's the way of the world, when you're young reeds amongst gnarled old trunks. Taletelling on the man had never been my plan, though. "Leave him and the others alone," I whispered.

"Why should I?"

I hated that my options were so few. I had but one card to play. "I'll give you what you want, instead."

"You?" He looked me up and down as if he couldn't believe what I might be offering. "Exactly what do you think I want?" One look into my eyes told him to drop the pretense of innocence. He licked his lips, squinted his piggy eyes, and said in a hush, "Why would you do that?"

"So that you'll let them be." That was the truth, plain and simple.

Again, he surveyed me, measuring the offer. "Swiftdare is more my type. Blond and pretty. Smooth. You're..." I raised my eyebrows, almost daring him to insult me. "You're dark. Your legs are furry. Your eyes are black and your ears are big. You look like a little monkey." I'd grown up hearing much worse. Certain he'd put me in my place, though, he smirked. "Why would I swap him for you?"

I leaned in and murmured directly into his ear. "Because I know exactly what I'm doing."

Involuntarily, he licked his lips. With a gulp, he nodded. "Follow me."

Cellarer Avery's domain lay at the *Beagle*'s tail end on the ship's middle deck, separated from the senior Brother's quarters by the refectory, equipment rooms, a large conference area grandiosely called the scriptorium, and a tiny chapel for the few brothers with actual religious beliefs. The Scholastic Brotherhood's culture honored the old monastic ways without replicating them; although the area in which the Brothers gathered for meals and end-of-day social activities was deemed the refectory, it was as bland and functional as a typical mess hall on any other transport ship. Past Compline, though—the traditional hour in which we all were supposed to be in our beds—the dining area was abandoned, the lights automatically dimmed by three-quarters.

"This way." Behind the serving line and into the kitchens he led me, pulling behind him the accordion-pleated hatch cover. "We'll be alone here. Now, let me see, let me see what I've won for myself."

I could scarcely object to his manhandling when I'd offered my body to him. Still, it was with aversion that I allowed him to draw up my nightshirt into a tangle over my head and expose my naked body from the neck down. His cold fingers prodded; they weren't slimy, but my skin crawled and shivered as if they were. From behind, kneeling down, he yanked apart my legs by the ankles, forcing me to spread wide. I felt stirrings of his breath upon my ass cheeks.

"Hairy...so hairy. We don't like that. No, we don't. But young." A rough hand stroked, then slapped my ass. "So young. No, leave it on." He meant my nightshirt, from which I was trying to extract myself. "Safer that way."

I compromised by allowing the garment to hang around my neck like a giant ruff. I wheeled around to face him, rolling the excess fabric beneath my chin. "If I let you..." I left unsaid the conclusion to that sentence. He knew what I meant. "You will leave all those kids below deck alone. Especially Swiftdare."

"Yes, yes." His tiny eyes glinted with impatience. I swiveled my hips away when he made a grab for my cock. "I promise."

Many would find fault with my choice, I know. Yet I justified it thusly: it saved a friend discomfort, and I took no personal satisfaction from what followed. When Avery planted loud kisses on my thighs and then up the length of my stiffening dick, its arousal was purely mechanical. No part of me relished the sight of him moistening his lips to an unwholesome sheen as they engulfed my swelling head. Friction and stimulus kept me hard. Not the repugnant sounds of his self-satisfied slurping, or the sight of his equipment projecting from his opened breeches.

His cock was vile to behold. Its bloated head dwarfed the skinny shaft, much like an overripe beech mushroom that weighed down a narrow stalk. More grotesque was the left turn it took halfway up the shaft. At full mast, his erection pointed to ten on an old-fashioned clock. He tugged at himself with such force I feared the man would cause himself damage.

No, I delighted neither in his attentions nor the sight of him, as his sallow cheeks bloomed scarlet from gobbling me in as far as he could. I shrank from his touch and cried out in pain when he dug his thumbnail into the cleft of my ass, then further into the hole itself. But I allowed him to continue because of the deal we had made. Men like Avery never lasted long, given access to what they wanted. Over the years, I'd found it easier to placate them swiftly and quietly, to keep them drained of both semen and desire before either could build up and render the men public nuisances.

Five minutes, and this would be over. Five minutes, and he could sleep sated while the others remained unmolested.

And myself? Well. I had made this sacrifice many times before. I had survived. I would survive Cellarer Avery.

"Turn around," he ordered. I obeyed, bracing my forearms against a food preparation table laden with sealed bricks of vat-grown salt fish and compressed plantains. In the morning, these would be unpackaged and served for breakfast. My nightshirt still hung around my neck, drooping over my chest and onto the provisions. I found it almost comforting to have my head and body so cleanly divided. Once again, he pried apart my legs, then knelt to seize the furry globes of my butt and force them high and wide. My dick jolted involuntarily when he buried his face between my cheeks to tongue the hole. Even that momentary pleasure he ruined, though, by complaining in a stage whisper, "Too much hair! Next time, shave."

No use retorting there'd be no next time. I'd have to repeat this scene every few days for the next two weeks until we reached Plum. Then I'd have to see what awaited us. I would refuse to shave, though. What I am doing is accommodation enough.

I gasped when he struggled to his feet and shoved me down onto the table. One sweep of his arm and the crates of salt fish went flying. They hit the kitchen floor with a thud. I, too, let loose a protest when I felt his enormous knob jutting against my hole with barely any lubrication. When he pinned me down against the cold metal, my right arm clawed out to slow him down, to push him off. That proved fruitless, so I braced for impact.

A cry escaped my lips the moment his wicked tool shoved itself in. I could not help myself. Though I've been penetrated by many cocks—some only tolerated, a few welcomed—without exception, they had been warm and pliant flesh. So rigid and unyielding was Avery, however, that I wondered if he had decided to eviscerate me with one of his kitchen implements. A cold stone pestle for my mortar, or a pegging with the handle of a metal spoon. But no, I knew it was his dick when my hole reached the turn in his shaft. My insides protested at the wayward path his twisted meat proposed to take and attempted to correct it by clamping down, but he won out in the end.

For the first time in more years than I could count, tears welled in my eyes. Pride forbade me to release them, but Avery knew they were there. He knew, despite the veil of nightshirt concealing my head from his view. "Oh, yes," he hissed, driving in once more. I so badly wanted not to yelp, not to let my distress be known, but every thrust drew from me an echo of animal lament that echoed around the kitchen's stark surfaces, a sharp keen my body could not help. "Quiet now," he said with a laugh, even as he pounded with more vigor to extract a reaction. "Don't wake anyone. Be a good boy."

Nigh upon passing out I was at a few points, so brutal was the pain of him. But again, pride and a resolution to endure what I had signed up for kept me from protest. I steeled my resolve, spread my legs wider, and permitted him to continue. In truth, I was not victim here, but volunteer. All I could think throughout the ordeal was better me than Swiftdare.

"Yes...yes. That's right, boy." Cellarer Avery's breath labored in his chest, ejecting itself in rasps and whines as he closes in upon his release. Louder and more violent he grew. Were the table not bolted to the floor, we both would be halfway across the kitchen by now. "Take my seed, you worthless shit. Take it." He lit into me with a torrent of abuse, none of it arousing to me, though it inflamed his own rutting.

I felt a wrenching in my guts as he unloaded. At least his ejaculate was warm as it coursed around the cold bone of his dick. Hands seized my ass to pull it apart so he could drive into me as deeply as possible. As one escaped tear coursed down my cheek, Avery thrashed and grunted until, at long last, he subsided and collapsed across my back, still planted inside. I prayed he would soon withdraw and end my agony.

Without warning, the hatch cover quietly pleated into an accordion as someone opened it from the outside. Into the aperture stepped Amodeo, shirtless yet still wearing his breeches. His half-disrobed state allowed him to accommodate a Heal-Me device into which he'd inserted his left forearm to the elbow—a portable model that could ameliorate small injuries, infections, and chronic illnesses. The Heal-Me's amber wrist display lit him from below, lending him the unearthly, golden appearance of an ancient religious icon. From it, he looked up, blinked with surprise, and met my eyes.

For an endless moment, we regarded each other. My face was red and streaked. His, a mask of incomprehension. The Prior's gaze flickered from me to Avery, who still heaved and wheezed where he had collapsed atop my spine, then back again. For a moment—a short moment to be sure, but no less painful for its duration—I thought I witnessed in his expression surprise, then disappointment. A curtain descended across his features that rendered them neutral. He backed out slowly, silently, breaking the lock our eyes maintained only when he turned to exit the refectory with hasty, silent steps, cradling the Heal-Me against his chest.

I should have wondered why the Prior, so hale, so full of life, needed such a device. To my discredit, I did not.

Whether from his post-coital haze or perhaps because my nightshirt had blocked his view, Cellarer Avery had not noticed Amodeo's silent entrance and exit. Nor did he make anything of the opened kitchen hatch. "Stay the night," he pleaded, as I extricated myself from his loathsome grip. But I refused and staggered out, making my escape to rinse myself in the latrine. There I used half my next day's water ration to get me to a state where I felt only one-quarter clean. By the time I limped back to the lowest deck, I at least no longer stunk of the man's spit and semen.

"What did you do?" Swiftdare uncurled himself from my mattress, where he'd lain since I'd sent him there. These soft settlement boys. How easily might I despise them for their uncomplicated upbringings, placid as a farm pond spared even the ripples from a thrown pebble. Yet Swiftdare's concern for my well-being seemed genuine. I could not help but be touched. He searched my face for answers. "Are you all right? Should I...?"

From another open cabin, I heard the gentle snoring of another initiate. I sat down beside Swiftdare. Too quickly, much to the discomfort of my brutally plundered fundament. "If Cellarer Avery distresses you again, you must let me know. Immediately. I will fix it."

"The things he tried..." Swiftdare gulped. "Beneath the covers. His hands..."

"I know. He will not bother you again."

"But what did you..."

"Don't ask." Swiftdare's limited experience could never let him imagine anything approaching the grim truth. Apprising him of the facts would make him miserable. I spoke with reassurance, as I might to one of the younglings back home. "He is gone. You should get some sleep. In your own bunk," I added, in case he had ideas of staying. I wanted to be alone.

Yet once beneath my blanket, I slumbered little. My hole ached from its stretching, something I'd ordinarily not mind. Had anyone else used me for his satisfaction and left me wanting, I might have pulled up my nightshirt and, under cover of dark, let one hand pinch and prod tender nipples and sore flesh alike. I might have moved the other up and down over my shaft while my imagination roamed. Soiled after Avery's onslaught, though, I would find no escape through self-pleasure.

Instead, I tossed and turned, in one moment ruing my choice, in the next finding consolation knowing it had spared several others my current shame.

I was startled the next day, during the daily briefing for senior Brothers and initiates, that Prior Amodeo addressed me during his lecture on Plum and its relation to other former Salice settlements. He had been wending his way through the rows of scriptorium desks at which we all sat when he stopped by mine, which I shared with Swiftdare. "Tell me, Brother Sorrowful," he said, for a moment inspecting the data tablet on which I had traced with my finger a quantity of tortured doodles. "When we speak of the Salix, to whom do we refer?" I prepared to stammer out a textbook response, but he added, "What did they look like, for example?"

"I..." I stammered, regardless. After our wordless encounter last night, had there been any trace of rebuke in his tone, any measure of chastisement, I might have broken down in shame. But his eyes were as kind as ever. I sensed his intention in singling me out lay not in humiliation, but in giving us both a chance to regain our footing. I swallowed and replied, "As a race, the Salix were extinct long before mankind pulled itself from its knuckles and stood upright. There are no images of them in any historical record."

He nodded, pleased at my summary. "Yet..."

"Yet in what few Salice hieroglyphs we have recovered, when they refer to themselves, it's as slender, stick-like figures with poles as limbs. Most Brotherhood researchers believe they were perhaps insectoid in nature. Like a praying mantis."

Amodeo continued his walk around our desk. "Most Brotherhood researchers do, indeed. With some justification, despite the lack of visual evidence. And what do you believe they looked like, Brother Sorrowful?"

What a novel, liberating sensation it was, a man of authority asking my opinion as if it might matter. In that moment, I felt a portion of the previous night's disgrace dissolve. I considered his question seriously, almost giddy to think my answer might be welcomed, even valued. "Reverend Father," I said, after reflecting a moment. "I think they looked like trees."

Amodeo nodded, looked around the room to see if my words had sunk in, and planted his hand between my shoulders. His pat meant more than approbation of my response. To me, it felt like mercy. *Et te absolvo*, it told me. So he might have said, had he either been a religious man or allowed himself the authority to pardon. *Worry not. All will be well.*

The memory of that touch got me through the two weeks that followed of painful assignations in the kitchens. Once the expedition landed upon Plum, I refused to continue the arrangement I had with our cellarer.

Then, Avery tumbled to his death on our second night, down the Great Road. There were whispers that I'd pushed him.

I did not. But often I wished I had.

DAY ELEVEN

During the days, we venture along the Great Road. We pick our way over the rubble and avoid nests of grubs. We rest upon the flat dark stones of the plinths. As we hike, we lob hypotheses like a ball in a game of catch. Perhaps the road had been built for transport, I venture, and Amodeo will ask me what was being moved, to and from where, and why. Or he suggests that it is possible we walk not upon a road at all, but atop the uppermost stones of a great wall that has become buried in dirt over the millennia. I point out the absence of any more stone beneath the interlocking rectangles on which we trod. Back and forth we volley until we are hoarse. At least it keeps us sane, for we are no closer to a destination than when we began.

Nights, we sometimes find it difficult to sleep. We make camp, we eat, we sit still at sunset, waiting for the chilling ruckus sure to come. When quiet falls, for protection, we place our bedrolls side by side. Lying on our backs, we stare at the almost silvery bellies of the fen bladders drifting high above us and beyond them, the stars in the violet sky. "Why did you choose me for this scouting trip?" I ask him.

When a fen bladder nears the end of its life cycle, at first its hanging tendrils begin to dry and fade, turning from green to the color of straw. No longer does it synthesize the hydrogen it needs to keep afloat; it will sink to the forest floor, then toughen and flatten into a hand-sized silver scale when depleted. These husks I've discovered I can gather, shave away their desiccated fronds, and adhere together using cypress sap, to form a tarpaulin of sorts that keeps us dry on nights when the bladder cover isn't as dense.

A solitary bladder nearing its expiration has drifted down from the mass above. It holds enough gas barely to keep it afloat, but not so much that it resists Plum's gravity. When I'd batted it earlier to keep it away from the fire, it had bounced aloft like a child's toy balloon before descending again. Now Amodeo and I take turns poking the wilting bladder whenever it comes close, amusing ourselves by seeing how long we can keep it airborne without the tendrils touching the ground. He seems to be hesitating over his reply. "You were the most qualified for a scouting mission. Obviously." I know him well enough now to recognize when he prevaricates. I also know that if I keep my mouth shut, he will continue talking. I'm proven right, after we bat the bladder into the air a few more times. "We were all in shock from the loss of Cellarer Avery and the others. Because you were close to him, I thought perhaps I should get you away from camp for a time."

I can't help but let a sigh of exasperation escape my lips.

"It was a fair assumption! When I happened upon the two of you...in the kitchens...together..." So. We are to discuss that night, after all. I truly hoped we might avoid the topic.

"Please..." I beg, drawing myself up. My last attempt to send the fen bladder heavenward goes awry; it floats behind us and sinks over the campfire. All at once, it catches alight. One second, a gout of bright flame, the next a scattering of ash. "It wasn't what you thought."

"Ayden," is his only mild reproach. He rolls onto his side and props up his head with a hand. "I loved a boy, once. I may be old, but my eyes recognize the significance of one man astride another. Even when it happens on a kitchen table." The question of which sex he might desire is somewhat answered, at least, I think with relief. "But you did not look happy that night. Did he hurt your heart? They said he had argued with you shortly before he died. Was it a lover's quarrel?"

Horrified, I recoil. "He was not my lover!" With ragged breath, I disclose what I'd told no one else. "He was a monster. I told him so the night he died. He had demanded I...satisfy him in the initiate's tent. He didn't care if the others saw or heard. He probably wanted them to see. To shame me. He was drunk. And mean. Then the noises started. At dark." I did not have to explain which noises. Amodeo knew exactly what I meant. "He dragged me outdoors. Told me he'd show me what a real monster looked like. I ran off in the rain, and he...he..."

"No. That is not a lover's quarrel." Amodeo's face is as stone. "But in front of the other initiates? Why would he humiliate you? Please. If you can, tell me."

I do not weep in front of the Prior, but my eyes and nose are moist as I uncork my tale. My bare forearm must suffice to wipe with. Because of the planet's warm temperatures, I have been relaxing without my tunic. My story spares nothing, from the Cellarer's nighttime encroachments to his abuse of Swiftdare and the bargain I made. Out it all tumbles. With every word, with every ugly secret I harbor unfurled and set free to float among the fen bladders overhead, I feel somewhat lighter in spirit. It is good to unburden. Better to have Amodeo as my confessor. But I still feel disgrace.

I await his verdict once I am done. During my abbreviated tale, he sits upright to face me. He appears older than he did nearly two months ago when he greeted me upon the *Beagle*'s drop dock; every fresh horror of my tale likely adds more gray hairs to his head. "Why did you not come to me at the time?" His soft plea seems to apportion much of the blame to himself. "Or even Brother Greywit, who was supposed to be keeping an eye on you initiates..."

My head shakes slowly. "It would have been Avery's word against mine. The man who keeps everybody fed versus a youth no one knew. I have not proved myself to any of you in any way! Why would you believe me?" Amodeo attempts to interrupt, but I have more to say. "The Brotherhood has its customs, and I have respected them all. I try to speak like you, act like you. You are idealistic, and I admire that. But the order is not so different from the world outside. And I know how the world works."

Amodeo visibly wrestles with himself. He starts to speak, then stops, shaking his head and working his lips. Again, he appears poised with a counterargument, but his eyebrows furrow and he holds a hand to his face. He stands, paces, and sits once more. Only after a considerable time does he speak. "I have failed you."

"No."

"Yes, Ayden. I have failed you. We all failed you. I cannot fault your compassion for Swiftdare, but the risk you took...Avery was a monster, and we let him loose among the lambs. I am so, so sorry." He crosses his legs to face me once more and reaches for my hands. Pressing them between his own, he stares into my eyes. "No harm will come to you again, while I am around. I swear it."

With relief, I laugh a little and allow him to squeeze my

hands more tightly. He has not judged me poorly, after all. "I can take care of myself."

"Oh, don't I know it!" The Prior's bark of laughter echoes among the cypress trunks. "You say you haven't proved yourself. But this camp. Our meals. How many times have you saved my heedless hide? We have survived on Plum by ourselves for ten days, you young idiot, all thanks to you. What more fucking proof do you require?"

He's wrong. Not for employing profanity, though it is the first coarse word I have ever heard the man utter. The Scholastic Brotherhood might not abjure the pleasures of the flesh or worldly interests, but they do attempt at all times to project an air of gentility. Not for calling me an idiot. I knew he said the word with affection.

No, I snub his praise because all the things that so impress him are the things children would do, among the Sovereign State clans. The grubbing for foodstuffs, the camp preparation, the boiling of water to make it potable—all the dozens of little tasks at which Amodeo seems to marvel are to me routine. Duties for the nonessentials, while the daddies and older brothers are out blowing things up and protecting our liberty.

So, I remain silent, refusing to take credit where none is due. I don't want to withdraw my hands from his, though. I redirect the conversation and venture a question. "May I ask about this boy you loved?"

Instantly, I regret my words, for he loosens his grasp to run his fingers through his hair. "Oh, Ayden. It was so long ago. I was much younger. And in prison, at the time, truth be told."

"In prison! What did you do?" Mine is not a polite question, I realize, but I am so astonished that I cannot help myself.

He laughs. "Corporate interference, not an act of violence. You see, for much of my adult life, I have suf-
fered from an infection of the blood. Without weekly
treatment, over time it could become debilitating. Fa-
tal." I nod, recalling the sight of him with his arm in
the Heal-Me. "I and others believed a particular Pharmafarm was withholding a real, actual cure for the
condition. Something that would eradicate it entirely.
But they concealed it. That way, they could force the
afflicted into a lifetime of expensive, ongoing therapy.
Maximum profits for them, in the end. We organized
boycotts. Got on the newsfeeds. The Settlements
courts sentenced me to three years for attempting to
silence corporate free speech rights. It was bullshit." I
thrill a little at this profanity-using, bad-boy side of
Amodeo. "I met him on Demios...the same place I
met you. The moon houses a prison complex buried in
its rock, as well as that jump station. Jonathon. That
was his name. Love at first sight, if you can find love
in an unhappy place." He smiles, lost in a happy remi-
niscence. "We would find ways to get ourselves assigned to the dirtiest jobs, so we could be together. No
one would check on a pair of inmates assigned to
muck out the sewer lines, so long as the work got
done."

"What did he look like?"

Part of me aches to hear the words, *like you*. That part is
immediately disappointed. "He was blond. A bit of a
tough. Tattoos all over. Had a reputation for fighting."
Amodeo speaks as a man not shackled by a memory but
pleased to be able to share it. "When we would talk
about what to do together after our release, he would
speak of joining the Scholastic Brotherhood. I'd never
heard of it. *Doesn't it sound nice, living out the rest of our
lives in peace and quiet?*, he'd say." He guffaws. "It did
sound nice. Well, to me, anyway."

"And what happened?"

"Oh." He grimaces. "He was only in for manslaughter, so he was free long before I. When I got out and began my postulancy, I supposed I hoped he'd join me." My fear is that Amodeo still holds a torch for his lost love, that he still yearns to find him somewhere among the far-flung Brotherhood chapterhouses, but his face has lost most of its misty nostalgia and longing. Once again, he speaks in his everyday voice. "Empty talk, all of it. I found out soon enough that he was incarcerated again. Murder, that time. I stopped checking on him, eventually. It was long ago, and I was a naive child. None of it amounted to anything."

"But you joined the order because of him." I wonder if he'd allow me to hold his hand again. "That's something. And look." I gesture to the cypresses encircling us and the bower of fen bladders above. "More peace and quiet than you can shake a stick at."

I love being able to make the man laugh. His merriment warms the little clearing more than my campfires. "Oh, my boy," he says, thrilling me. Then he grows still and serious. "Ayden. I am beginning to worry that we...have been abandoned."

"Stop." His words send me into a panic, but I don't let it show.

He nods. "I am losing my optimism. And I...I need a working Heal-Me."

No, no. This is not good. Heart sinking, I dare to ask, "How many treatments have you missed?"

"Two. Yesterday and the week before."

I can fix this, somehow. I cast around for ideas. "We'll return to the landing site."

He shakes his head. "Our Heal-Me was the first thing I looked for when we found the camp abandoned. It may have been in use when they fled on the shuttle." Sensing my panic, he rests a hand on my forearm. "Ayden, I will not kick the bucket tomorrow. Weeks or months might pass before I felt any effects. But the longer I delay cleansing my blood, the higher my chances of other infections. And we are in a strange world..." He raises his palms to the skies, helpless.

I have only thought of the Prior as a man of courage. A leader. I have been relying upon his good cheer to weather us through this predicament. Never would it occur to me that he might need to lean upon me, instead. Well, fine. I will be the sturdy companion he needs. "We will not abandon hope," I tell him. "Protocol demands the ship search for us."

"But it has been...nearly a fortnight. This planet is big and we are so small."

One of us must remain firm. "They search for us right now. They await a sign." I echo his words from before. "A sign will be delivered."

He presses two fingers against his forehead and winces. "You're right. I succumb to my doubts. Bah." He uses a stick to stir the embers of our fire nearby, then tosses it atop the pile. "Your beard is much like his. Jonathon's."

My what? "I don't have a beard," I reply, bewildered. For a moment, I wonder if his ailment causes hallucinations.

"You may not have the benefit of a mirror," he says, laughing. "But you haven't shaved in a long time. Plus, you are a naturally hairy young man. You have a beard, Ayden." He leans forward to rub my face. What I'd been thinking of as the scruff of a day or two riffles audibly beneath his fingertips. I'm surprised when I touch myself to find how long it's gotten.

Yet my companion's beard has flourished, too. He always maintained a very short stubble, but now it has blossomed into a forest of auburn growth, gray at the chin. On impulse, I reach out to cup his cheek and jaw with my palm.

He does not object to my touch. We stare into each other's eyes, our poses nearly mirroring the other. "Amodeo," I whisper.

The man pulls me in, using both hands to surround my cheeks, and kisses me deeply. Into his embrace I melt with such enthusiasm that he rocks backward onto his bedroll. I fall atop him, refusing to break the connection of our lips. Together grinds the growth of ten days of beard. I relish the burn.

I have wanted this man since the moment I saw him. A vague yearning at first, perhaps even a wish that someday in the future, I might cut half as dashing a figure as the man I'd seen on Deimos, bold as a pirate aboard the deck of the *Beagle*. Had I not desired him, I would not have experienced so deep and cutting a shame as when he'd caught Avery rutting me. I yearned for his approval. Like a trusty Labrador, I'd trotted alongside him day after day, growling at dangers, fetching, and wagging my tail.

Never did I imagine this might be the pat on the head that I would ultimately receive.

Though we had taken short rainwater showers late in the afternoon, we both smell of sweat and sun. Having nothing but dirty field clothes to wear will do that. Nonetheless, I press my crotch into his, then savor the sensation of stiffness against stiffness, of his hardened flesh urgent against my own. Not until tonight had I known he preferred his own sex, much less felt any desire for me. Yet just as I begin freeing myself from doubt and allowing myself to enjoy the taste of his mouth, still sweet from sponge fruit, he pushes me away.

"No," he whispers. "We can't." Upon his back, he holds me at arm's length, staring up. I have always thought of the Prior as a strong man, tall and solid like the sturdiest tree, unbowed by wind or storm. In this moment, though, he shakes his head slowly. Sorrow darkens his eyes. I've never seen him so vulnerable.

My own unruly mop hangs around my face. I nod with vigor. "Oh, yes. We must."

"I would not be an Avery." Now I understand. He hesitates not from lack of desire, but simple fear. "Ayden, you are so young. And I..."

"You are everything, in my eyes." Even as he searches for ways to dissuade me, I loosen the ties at his tunic's bottom and slip it from his shoulders. Then I begin unfastening his breeches. "Since we began walking this road together, all I've wanted is to look at you. To be near you." He shakes his head, laughing with embarrassment, but I hold his face in my hand so he must see the truth. My index finger rests along his faded scar. "I've wanted this. I am old enough to know my own wishes."

"I should not take advantage of one so young."

Even he does not believe his own protests. "Then I must take advantage of you, old man."

When I press my bearded chin into the tender flesh at the base of his rib cage, he gasps. His hands fly skyward, but he no longer stops me. Hungrily, I explore the chest I have admired for days. My cheek rubs up his sternum, fur against fur. My hands have already seized his waistband and begun to tug it lower, sliding down the hips, catching on something stiff and unyielding. I know exactly what organ hinders my urgency to disrobe him; my greedy fingers reach to grasp it, to claim it as my own.

But with surprising force, he seizes my wrist before I achieve my goal. All his doubts now evaporated, once again he kisses me hungrily. His tongue dives deep, exploring my mouth as if scouring a new world for its secrets. Our combined center of gravity shifts as he rises and pushes me backward. Together we fall upon my own bedroll. Now he is atop me, grinding into my hip with his unsheathed hardness. Through his nose, he breathes heavily, huffing for air. I fancy I can feel the tendrils of the fen bladders, dipped low above, tickling my skin. It is only his hair, teasing sensitive flesh.

In one fluid motion, he divests himself of the tunic. For a moment, a vision of finely aged muscle and sinew kneels above me. I am treated to only the briefest glimpse of his cock, thick and threatening, as he shoves his trousers down to his thighs. As he presses against me, I feel it stabbing below my abdomen. His dick seems to want to create a new hole there, so insistently does it poke and prod as he gathers me into his arms. How I wish I could grow one to suit him.

Amodeo's hands are everywhere, all at once. Squeezing my shoulders, running through my tangles, tracing my face as if memorizing every feature. For the first time, my own palms are able to slide upon the curves of his mighty arms, over the man's mountainous shoulders, into the valley at the small of his back, then once again up the inclines of his backside. When he wrenches his lips away from mine to kiss my ear, my jaw, the tip of my chin, I gasp; his mouth travels down my neck to my clavicle, where he scrapes his coarse facial hair from one side to the other. In the wake of that fire, he soothes my skin with more slow kisses.

I'd removed my top before we had settled down to talk, but that's not enough for him. As he scuffs his rough whiskers from nipple to nipple, he fumbles for the fastenings of my breeches. So anxious is he to remove them that he lifts high my narrow frame with a single hand.

"Ow, ow, ow," I complain, causing him to hesitate. I make him wait, my hips still thrust into the air, while I dig under my waistband and withdraw my arc dagger. Luckily, it's in its scabbard and I've left the safety on. I toss it onto the ground.

His eyebrows rise in comical surprise when once again I begin fumbling beneath the sash. This time I produce my homemade slingshot. When, after another quick search, I pull out a pair of billiard nuts—they're good ammunition—he blinks. "And I thought you were just happy to see me."

"Keep going," I growl.

Relieved of my arsenal, Amodeo releases the stretchy material around my waist and thighs. As he lowers me back onto my shoulders, he helps me shed the last of that tight outer skin. Save for a cuff still stubbornly clinging to my left ankle, I lie naked before the man.

I've no time to relish the sight of him. Again, I only get the briefest of glimpses of his cock in silhouette against the campfire beyond. My pulse quickens at the bobbing shadow. The man wrenches apart my legs, flips me over, and inserts his knees between mine. I exhale what air remains in my panting lungs as he lands atop me, then gasp as his chest hair grazes my soft skin. I cry out at the sensation of his wet lips upon the back of my neck, then shiver as they sojourn past my hairline. Hot breath singes my ears; my hands claw into the moss when he bites hard into my earlobe. "You want this," he reminds me with a growl.

I do. I want nothing more than eternally to feel the weight of the man atop me. Never will I regret how he plants my arms high above my head so that he can attack first one armpit, then the other, with his lips and tongue. At first, I find myself muffling my exclamations, so accustomed am I to hiding any desire in close quarters. Yet stifling my groans into the bedroll fails to satisfy. The planet of Plum needs to know how glorious this man makes me feel. The fen bladders above stir as I curl back my neck, raise my face to the heavens, and let loose a roar of pleasure.

Amodeo's midsection quivers against me as he chuckles. His arms embrace me from behind. "What are you doing, silly boy?"

I flip onto my back and pull him atop me. "We are alone on this world. The only living creatures we've seen for days are the grubs. Let us be loud." Seeing the doubt in his eyes, I add, "Haven't you ever been so happy you could howl?"

"I have. I am," he amends. I grin at him in invitation. Upon his face I see writ plain the question, *should I?*

At my nod, he too raises his head and bays. Above, masses of bladders shift and slowly glide, parting briefly to show us a glimpse of the stars. Somewhere out there lies home. But we are here, upon the soft carpet of moss of this planet, bounded by the rock of the Great Road on one side and the unending forest of cypresses on the other. Rousing the notice of the sunset noise's source may be unwise, I know. But for once, let our commotion frighten whatever makes them. Perhaps to whatever passes for its ears, the ferocity of our lovemaking makes it shiver in dread.

Once more, his mouth moves down my torso, ravaging my belly, scraping hard against my pelvic bone. His hand grips my dick, squeezing it both to satisfy my urgency and make me yearn for more. I'm shy about my hygiene, briefly. A week and a half it's been since I had the benefit of either a sonic scrubber or even something as primitive as soap. To him, I must taste good; however, for he consumes the length of me in one go, gobbling my stiff flesh to the root. I let my pleasure be known with a bellow. Amodeo stares up at me with lidded eyes, lost in his own private delight.

I do not surrender to Amodeo in exchange for information, or protection, or to protect others. For perhaps the first time in my life, I give myself to a man because he wants me and because I want him. I am almost loath to let him continue, so unused am I to accepting this intense an attention with no transaction in the offing. Yet I'm helpless to convince him to stop.

His fingers tug hard at my balls, multiplying every sensation. When I try to shift so that I might do something to enhance his own enjoyment—to stroke his hair, perhaps, or squeeze his nipples—he brushes away my hands. I get the impression that if he could, he'd strap me down and force me to enjoy his wet lips, his warm mouth, his welcoming throat. My member is not the largest, but he worships it as if nothing else matters. I am too shaken to the core to protest.

There comes a point when he pushes himself up from his prostrate attitude and stares at me with a feral intensity that makes my cock leap. Saliva streaks his mouth and beard, but he doesn't bother to wipe his face. "Do you want to make me happy?" he asks.

He knows my answer, but I rasp out a yes and nod wildly. It's still too dark for me to see what stands from between his thighs, but as he looms closer, I can feel it bobbing and nudging. My knees begin to draw up involuntarily, so badly do I want him. With his own weight, he pushes them back down.

I stare into his eyes as he lifts a hand to his mouth. Into his pinched fingers he releases a quantity of the spit he's worked up, before moving them downward between his legs. To my surprise, however, he applies the makeshift lube not to his own cock, but to mine. From toes to the crown of my head, I shudder, twitching as he pinches the sensitive head. His hand returns to his mouth, lingers, then delivers a second payload to my rigid flesh. Then once more. But this time, he leans forward slightly to apply the moisture to his hole.

Another novelty for me. I am unaccustomed to a man desiring me this way. Yet that doesn't mean I'm not pleased. I can only gaze at him with adoration as he scoots forward and quirks his mouth in a cheeky nod to our predicament. Then he grows more serious as he raises his hips, positions himself above me, and lowers himself.

A hiss escapes his mouth as I feel nothing but pressure on the tip of my cock. I am such a novice at this variation of the act that I can only lie there, helpless, as he attempts to engulf me. He bites his lip, grimaces, and tries again, this time grasping my shaft from below. "It's been so long," he admits, half-apologizing. "I'm too tight."

"There's no haste," I remind the man. I want to add that he doesn't have to continue. Not to please me. I would have been content to kiss him and press myself against his body all night.

But this coupling is what he desires. Again, I feel warmth and pressure at the very pinnacle of my cock. Then a parting. I cry out at feeling an inch or two of myself enveloped with warm, soft tissue. Amodeo gasps; a smile suffuses his face as he gazes with wonder at me. "Cleave unto me," he whispers.

Down he slides, surrounding my cock with heat. Silky flesh clings fast to my own. He absorbs me, centimeter by centimeter, until I am finally part of him. My lips tremble. In some overwhelming, nearly mystical way, I feel greater than my own petty self. My fears, my jealousies—every inconsequential dissolves in the face of what we create as he rocks atop me, ass to cock.

Cleave unto me, he had said, and some part of me had rolled my eyes at another imperative couched in florid

Brotherhood anachronisms. Yet, cleave I do, with a ferocity that may never separate us.

Like acrobats, we intertwine fingers and press our palms together as he rises and falls. We can counterbalance the other this way as our hips thrust and parry. There's a fierceness in his grin; he bares his teeth in a snarl that mellows to delight whenever he reaches my base. And now, finally, I can see his mighty cock as it swings above. Firelight throws into relief the thick veins that highlight its skin; the man is much larger than I, as I suspected. I'd seen him soft during our bathing sessions and knew him to be thick and hooded. Yet I'm unprepared for the club-like erect monster bobbing so close, or for its sheer weight as it slaps my abdomen on the downstroke.

Goo flows freely from the tip that protrudes from beneath his tight foreskin. Strands of it adhere to my stomach, then stretch like rubber bands when he ascends. I want to grab that beast, to see how far my fingers might reach around its girth. He squeezes my hands too tightly with his own, however. Nor would I wish to release them, while we cleave this first time. The intimacy of our clasped fingers makes me feel toward him as I might a sweetheart, though we fuck more like wild animals upon the forest floor.

"I'm not hurting you, am I?" he asks after a few particularly savage twists of his hips. Genuine concern softens his eyes.

"No," I assure him. "It's amazing." With his help, I pull myself up for a lingering kiss, though we dare not break our connection. "But am I...making it good for you?" He stares at me with incomprehension. "I know you're doing most of the work, but...it's my first time. Penetrating a man, I mean."

He blinks several times before comprehension dawns. "Oh, Ayden." He lets loose my hands so he can bend over and kiss me. I raise my hips to remain buried deep in the velvet depths of his hole. "I did not suspect. Truly." He grins at me, proud. "I wouldn't have guessed. You are doing it so right." He surrounds my head with his hands and covers my face with soft, sweet pecks.

"You're happy?"

"I am very, very happy." My cock swells at his assurance, making him close his eyes and groan. "Don't ever stop making me happy."

"Will you make me happy sometime, too?" While he leans atop me, I begin thrusting from below, resuming the labor he'd been so willing to perform until now. His hands straddle my neck, as if he's at the apex of a push-up. "Will you cleave unto me?"

Only half-grasping what I'm asking him through my pounding upon his prostate, he stares down. "You would enjoy that?" With vigor, I nod. "I worried to ask it of you, after...after the pain caused by..."

I appreciate what name he's trying not to say, in the moment's heat. "I want you in me, as much as I want to stay inside you."

Both he and his cock nod in agreement. Now, for the first time, I reach out to grasp it. It burns hot as a welding iron. "My illness should not be transmittable, if that worries you..."

"That's the last of my worries. I want this big, fat dick deep inside me. Repeatedly. Every day, if you can manage it, old man."

That challenge allays his fears. His jaw sets in comic determination. "Oh, I can. And shall."

"I'll hold you to it." Spurred on by our banter, our mouths search for the other. I have to withdraw from him as I straighten out the bedrolls and reposition him onto his back, but it's only temporary. I take a moment to relish the sight of that gaping aperture, slippery and glistening in the firelight. "Feel it," I demand. When he doesn't instantly obey, I pull one hand between his legs and force the fingertips into the cavity. "Feel right there. Where we connected. Observe how wide open you are, Reverend Father."

He has his knees pulled up to his shoulders. My words inspire him to shove two fingers inside himself. His jaw drops in awe. "Oh, Initiate. I am agape."

I nod, suddenly cocky. "I did that."

He nods with fervor. "You did."

"Do you want more?" My dick is no match for his, but poised for plunder, it swells to proportions I've never before seen. "Tell me," I demand, when he only bobs his head some more.

"I want your dick in me, Brother." As much as the words thrill me, I'm even more aroused as he employs my name. "Fuck me, Ayden. Ayden, please. Fuck me."

I shove myself back in and am rewarded by a sharp grunt from deep in his gut, and a widening of his eyes.

Another storm begins clattering above us as I hold high his legs and drive myself in. Raindrops tap against the fen bladders in a tattoo like a thousand distant snare drums. In the distance resonates one of Plum's infrequent rolls of thunder, lower than either bass drum or timpani, more vibration than sound. Soon, the plash of water drowns out our own brute snarls. From time to time, the bladders part and allow raindrops to splatter upon my makeshift tarpaulin, or to fall with a hiss into the fire, but we are too lost in the other to notice. We only have this one first time together, and I intend to commit every sensation to memory.

I am younger than he, however, and my stamina is not so practiced in this position that I can last forever. My partner hoists high his legs, spreading them wide to open himself. Boy I may be, but I perform our dirty deed with the vigor and confidence of a man. Amodeo's eyes roll upward beneath leaden lids, leaving visible only the whites. Every part of his body quivers; electrical impulses galvanize his skin, his muscles jump, his nipples harden into ingots. I possess the power to excite him. To make his cock surge and swell.

The sight inspires me to find new ways to make him react. A new angle from which to plunge, a whisper of encouragement that might flame his fires. I grasp his erection like a saddle horn, using the searing flesh for balance as together our hips rise and fall. The new sensations push me quickly to the brink, however. "I am close," I warn.

"Let loose," he begs. With effort, he holds open his eyes to regard me with wonder. "Be part of me." The words spur me forward. "Deep inside. Come for me, Ayden."

Moist from a mixture of sweat and spittles of rain, I drive in, again and again. Some impulse prompts me to seize him by the hairy calves and to rest them upon my shoulders. Never did I suspect this side of myself: assertive, dominant. From nowhere it arises. Idly, I wonder if and where it might retreat, once I am done.

Again, I roar, lifting my voice to the heavens. With wordless joy, I celebrate the sensations that course from spine to dick then onward, deep into Amodeo. I baptize him with fire. He gasps, feeling the molten connection between us. His own hands fumble and grasp for my hips to draw me in, to hold me there while I release everything I have to share.

He relieves me of my grip upon his cock. While tremors still possess me, his hand flies up and down over its length. Soon, he, too, bawls out his excitement, laden with profanities. His hole grips me, vice-like, as semen jets upon his chest, his shoulder, the tip of his chin. His lids narrow to slits; he regards me as if from far away.

I am now a part of him, I realize. My very essence, inside him.

The act's conclusion clears my head for a moment. As the noise of rushing blood subsides, replaced by the gentle rustle of the diminishing rain, however, doubt assails me. How will this change us? I shrink to consider how the moment's closeness might evaporate, now our passion is sated.

But Amodeo only shakes his head, sighs, and smiles. "Come here, you marvel," he murmurs, pulling me close. My cock slithers out of him, causing us both to gasp in disappointment.

Separate though we may now be, our bodies remain in sync. Swiftly, we negotiate a new position, facing each other, lying upon our sides, glued by his seed. His arms surround me as I nestle in the safety they afford. He toys with my hair. Plants a kiss atop my head. "I have never seen you look so happy as when you came."

Suddenly shy, I bury my face into the forest of chest fur tickling my nose. "Maybe I haven't been happy in a long while."

His knuckles bounce over the ridges of my spine. Malnourished I may no longer be, but in places, my bones still protrude. "Plum suits you."

Sleepy, I burrow against him. I'm surprised to consider that he's correct. Plum does suit me. After years crowded into bunkers, into cells, into chapterhouses bustling with activity, I relish this sleepy planet, heavy with cypress shade and soft with moss. It's a world no less fraught with dangers than those I'd known before, but here upon Plum I rest in the arms of the man I most crave and admire. And I am happy in our solitude. My belly rises and falls, amused at the thought.

I could remain here forever, absolutely. Amodeo, however, cannot. Plum will become his grave if we are stranded upon it for too long. No matter how warm and cozy I feel, that realization casts a shadow across our intertwined forms.

His drowsy fingers twiddle at my hairline. "Sorrowful no more, then." At my questioning huff, he explains. "You'll have to change your name."

I go along with his teasing. "Will I?"

"Mmm-hmm. We all do, at some point. No one expects you to keep your postulant's name forever. What will it be? Brother Hardpecker? Brother Amorous?"

"Those are amazingly terrible suggestions." With tenderness, I kiss the fool until he's quiet. "Let's just say the nature of my metamorphosis has yet to be determined."

But I need to determine it, and soon.

DAY THIRTEEN

Tonight, I'm face down, chin abutting the ground and seeing stars with Amodeo thrusting atop me, when I experience a vision of an old-fashioned hourglass. The object rests atop the road stone we're using as a table. It isn't close to empty, but its sands still fall at a steady pace. I know that someday the upper globe will release the last few grains. Time will come to an end. Not now. Not tomorrow. But someday.

"Let me make you mine," growls Amodeo into my ear, drawing me back to the here and now. I nod, breathless both from his weight and from the pounding he gives me. "Do you want my seed inside?"

"Please," I manage to beg. The sides of my face prickle with heat. Already, the man's insistent hammering at my prostate has reduced me to a compliant jelly. I feel his hands seizing my hips, his thick bush abrading my stretched and sore opening. Yet still he tries to shove deeper, thrust harder, to make a more profound impact upon my hole than anyone ever has.

I know he hopes to erase all the bad times I'd endured with one magnificent act of intimacy. For the most part, it's working. Yet no matter how tight his embrace, no matter how wonderful he makes me feel—no matter how happy I am to carry his essence even as he still holds my own—those sands still sift downward, accumulating speck by speck in a rising pile.

Afterward, when we hold each other by the campfire, he brushes the hair from my face and rearranges my beard into less of a mess. "I didn't hurt you, did I?"

"No!" I laugh. Quite the opposite. I've never had it so good. "Why would you even ask?"

"You just seemed distant. At the end, there. If you ever need me to stop..."

"I don't!" Now that the nightly rains have ceased, the whole planet seems poised at a standstill. There's no sound to be heard save for the hollow tapping noises of the bladders high above as they gently collide with each other. That is, other than his breathing, the crackle of the fire, and his contented sigh. "I didn't mean to be distant. I had thoughts."

"Thoughts of...?"

"I was thinking...between your satchel and mine are enough metal fasteners. If I set my arc dagger to low, I could create a handful or two of metal shavings." I am both sated and sleepy enough that my mouth works unimpeded. I've become less guarded around Amodeo now that I no longer have to hide my yearnings. "Cypress sap is a fairly good fixative, and I'm willing to bet it would harden under the right circumstances. I'd need to concoct some kind of fuel...I don't know if the two of us can produce enough waste to create the amount of saltpeter we'd need. Maybe the grubs..."

His eyebrows have risen steadily throughout my musings. "The grubs?"

"Saltpeter used to be made from bat guano, long ago. I'm wondering if the grubs...I haven't seen their poop, but we haven't gone looking for it, either. Their casings must be substantial. If we start stockpiling..."

"How fared your expedition to Plum, Reverend Father?" Amodeo alternates between a lighter, higher-pitched voice and his own as he carries on an imaginary dialogue. *"Quite well, Brother. Thank you for asking. Oh, capital, Reverend Father, and your research? Most enlightening, Brother. I spent my time stranded away from modern amenities, but at least I could pass the time collecting the poop of the planet's giant worms.* Remind me why," he continues, as he props himself upon an arm, "we are discussing grub poop and metal shavings and saltpeter and..." He pushes himself upright to face me. "Wait. Are you building a *bomb?*"

"No! Well, yes. But no! Not a bomb. A slow-release waterproof explosive."

"I cannot believe that while I was giving you the best rogering of your life..." I raise my eyebrows at his cocky assertion and assume a doubtful wince, but I only tease. He swats at me, as I intended. "Oh, yes, the *best* rogering of your life, you were coyly lying there and thinking about how to build a bomb. No." He holds up a hand when I try to interrupt. "Not a bomb. A slow-release waterproof explosive. How do you even know these things?"

"Everybody knows how to build a bomb."

"No, Ayden, they do not. I do not. No one of my acquaintance knows how to build a bomb. That is a skill set unique to you and your fiendish upbringing. For what purpose are we sacrificing our satchel clasps to build explosives?"

I sit up to explain. "More of a flare, really. If the *Beagle*... I mean, since the *Beagle* is looking for us, they need a sign. Just as you said. Now, I don't know what equipment they have on board." Amodeo shakes his head, though I'd hoped he might be able to fill me in. "But so far, they have not traced us along the road by day or found us or our campfires by night."

"The vessel is made for jumping and transport, not re-connaissance," muses Amodeo. "It may have the ability to search the surface for significant heat signatures, yet we might be too small."

"But if we were to stop traveling the road, set up a permanent camp, then make a large..."

"Bomb."

"...*flare* that wouldn't be hindered by the rains, and set it upon one of the Great Road platforms to burn at night..."

"Oh. I see." I have ignited a spark of optimism behind the Prior's eyes. "Several flares, to be certain. Perhaps even set upon multiple platforms. Yes. Yes. The ship would be searching for an anomaly. Something unusual that could arise only from us. How much of this poop would we need to collect?"

"A lot," I admit.

"Fine, fine. We can begin tomorrow. We'll find and trail a grub pack and observe where they leave their, ah, leavings. And how long before we can turn it into saltpeter?"

He is animated, alive. Making plans. Though he'd never held back during our coupling, ever since the man had confessed his doubts about our rescue, I have noticed a certain resignation in his demeanor. My suggestion has him anticipating adventure once more, and it wrecks me to disappoint him. "Months," I admit, miserable. When he stares at me for confirmation, I nod. "It takes a very long time."

"All right, then." I have to give him credit. Amodeo doesn't crumple. He takes a long inhalation and merely says, "Ah. Well. We will put this plan in the long-term survival column, then."

I butt the top of my head against his chest and am re-warded by his large, warm hands cradling it. "Amodeo. How much time do we have?"

I feel a soft kiss upon my crown. "I cannot tell you, love." He rests his head atop mine. "If I'm cautious, many months. Perhaps even a few years. The longer the infection builds without cleansing, the riskier it be-comes. It is not a pretty death, though. I will go blind, become deaf, lose my wits." His words leave me frozen. "But I have been thinking. If I begin to go downhill, I will spare you the pain..."

I sit up so abruptly I risk banging my skull into his. "No."

"...and spare myself the humiliation..."

"Not a word more. We will not come to that!" Is this how he spends his nights? Contemplating how undigni-fied his death here might be? Planning when and how to make his own exit? How terrified he must be be-neath that stoic exterior. And how badly I want to fix things and protect him. Neither of us has been com-pletely forthcoming with the other during our lovemak-ing. While I have plotted to make my explosives, he has had to blueprint his own demise. "Amodeo." Cupping his jaw, I turn his face to mine. "We will not."

"Fine." He concedes with a nod. "We will not come to that, if you say so."

"Fine. I do." I feel as if we've had our first argument somehow, though no voices have been raised. "We will find a way off Plum. And then," I threaten, "I'm never letting you out of my sight."

With a furious whisper, he assures, "That would be no punishment, Ayden." Amodeo pulls me into his sturdy arms once more. "Not for me."

"Nor I," I say into his chest, as I wonder what a future with him might look like. How many planets could we investigate, given a chance? "Would they allow us to stay together?"

"If we chose." He strokes my hair. "The Scholastic Brotherhood with many uranian couples within its ranks. There are no rules against it, though we're all expected to carry on with our duties or our scholarship. On board the *Beagle,* we had two..."

Interesting a topic as this might be for another day, I jerk up again with a sudden thought. "Smoke."

"What? Oh. You're making more bombs in your head, again. Really, lad, you make an old man doubt his charms when your mind wanders off so easily."

"Listen. We have one long-term plan."

"Grub poop." He truly enjoys repeating that phrase.

"We need another for the shorter term. So, we build a bonfire alongside the road. Fire might not catch their attention from orbit, but smoke might. Lots of it. We will feed a fire with damp wood. We wouldn't have to wait until dark, even. Keep it going from dawn until nightfall."

"Smoke would definitely be an anomaly. Stretch one of your tarps above, maybe," Amodeo suggests. "That would dissipate the smoke even more, perhaps give the embers some shelter." He chews a little at the side of his hand, thinking. "Experiment with some of the brush and leaves, to see if anything changes the smoke's color. Or density. Hmmm. How wide would you estimate those platforms to be? Ten, twelve meters?"

I cannot fashion a Heal-Me for the man from twigs and thickets, nor can I immediately improve our situation. But I've given Amodeo a gift in the form of hope. As he chatters on, tossing out possibilities and masterminding our solution, I watch his face glow and his youth return in the campfire's light. I make him no empty promise, but a vow. No more will we fret and plot in private. From now on, we will be a united front. Unto each other we have cleaved, after all.

When I look down between my crossed legs, I see my cock steadily rising, recovered from its earlier efforts. "Amodeo." I interrupt his spoken monograph on the creation and maintenance of dense smoke using locally sourced, sustainable planetary assets. "Amodeo," I repeat, clearing my throat.

He blinks several times, then seems to remember I'm there. "I'm sorry. Was I pondering aloud?" I nod, leaning closer. The faintest of smiles flickers upon his lips as mine draw near. "What's so important, my lad?"

"This." I take his hand and move it to my stiff dick, and am gratified to see his lids narrow with pleasure as he wraps his fingers around me to squeeze. "Tomorrow we begin our project, but this is your assignment for tonight."

"I see." He swallows hard. "I hope I prove an apt pupil, sir."

As he prostrates himself before me, I open my legs and knot my fingers among his curls. I can honestly say that the last thing on my mind, in the moment, is bombs.

DAY FIFTEEN

Liberty Day is what we celebrated on February fourteenth, growing up. The anniversary of our Sovereign Fathers bombing Raleigh and Columbia a hundred years before my birth. When I was a youngling, we'd start the holiday with the clan elders giving tedious speeches on—of course—Liberty and her archnemesis, Tyranny. Penance before pleasure, the mamas and daddies would say.

In a good year, there would follow taffy pulls and apples from storage, set on sticks and candied; in leaner times, potato pies and roasted parsnips. Those who could play instruments made music for all to dance. Sweethearts would exchange handcrafted cards with cupids and hearts—even the young men, who weren't usually encouraged in such indulgences. All day, one's ears would ring from the retort of homemade firecrackers. It wasn't uncommon for children to lose fingertips to their explosions. My two eldest brothers had only thirteen and a quarter fingers between them.

What I liked most about the holiday, the years we were able to spend the day aboveground, were the bonfires. While mamas and aunties worked on the food and daddies and clan leaders smoked their briar pipes and bragged about their boys, we younglings would gather branches and brush and pile them high. The very littlest would spend the day cutting paper hearts of wastepaper scavenged from relinquished office blocks and half-burnt homes—hundreds of them, snipped from abandoned personnel files, yellowed newsprint, and old returns from the immoral thing called the income tax. At night, the daddies would light the bonfires and we'd all cheer, then for hours the youngest would shower the fire with hearts that would turn to ash before they even reached the flames.

"The hearts represented the deaths of the oppressors," I explained to Amodeo. "Annihilated on the flames of righteousness."

He blinked at me. "You mean the seated lawmakers your people assassinated in organized terrorist attacks, you little ghoul?"

He was right, of course, but a younger me wouldn't have phrased it so baldly. Those atrocities had happened three generations before I was even conceived. I'd grown up not knowing anything but what I was taught. Later, when I found out the rest of the world celebrated a different holiday on February fourteenth, one that included the candy and cards but curiously omitted any sermonizing about cutting the throats of despots, I naively assumed United Settlements had stolen it from us and watered it down.

Today might be a new Liberty Day for Amodeo and myself, whatever the calendar date. Truth be told, though I keep a positive face for my companion's sake, I doubt that our one bonfire is going to nudge the needle. But it's a start.

All the previous day, Amodeo had stockpiled wood for burning, using his arc blade to cut old, weathered branches from the forest floor into logs we could carry to the Great Road. Then he had turned his attention to greener, damper, fresh shoots still attached to the trees;

these would create the smoke and steam we hoped might attract the *Beagle*'s attention. I scoured the same mossy expanse for bladder husks, sacrificed the cup from my mess kit to boil cypress sap into an adhesive that hardened, and expanded the larger of our two tarps to act as a bonfire lean-to. Sweaty and exhausted, we'd managed to transport most of the wood to the flat, black, pedestal-like stone adjacent to the road that was closest to our now-permanent camp. Then we'd returned home before the terror of sunset.

The tarp did its job of mostly keeping yesterday's work undisturbed by the elements. This morning, we erect the lean-to by tying the tarp to sticks with strips of cloth yielded from my tunic's sleeves, then stabilize the base with stones. The hutch's purpose is not so much to cover the bonfire as to shelter it against winds from the west. More small stones form a circle atop the plinth to contain the pile of brush, twigs, and dried leaves we pile within it, then a column of dry sticks to capture the initial flames.

I cede to Amodeo the honor of lighting the result of our hard labor, once we've laid the foundation. "Here's to environmental pollution in the name of rescue," he says grandly, holding his arc blade aloft. Both hands clutching the hilt just below the guard, he lowers the tip into the accumulation of timber and scrap and squeezes off the safety while I applaud.

I hear the familiar sound of an electronic major scale playing upward to indicate the blade activating—and after, the same scale downward, indicating an immediate power-off. I catch a flash of brightness as the arc attempts to complete itself, but nothing happens. Amodeo squeezes again. Another pair of rising and falling trills. Not even a spark. And not a recharger in sight.

"Must have exhausted the battery cutting all that lumber." He sounds mournful as he replaces the blade at his side. Without comment, I hand over my arc dagger so he can try again. This time, with less ceremony, he succeeds.

Neither of us says aloud what we're both obviously thinking: without the arc blade, we lack an efficient way to chop through larger fallen branches. We'll have to put our backs into it. That would be fine—except that also without the blade, the only weapon we have between the two of us is my little dagger. And my slingshot, I suppose.

We haven't needed them for defense before. If we can get the smoke signals noticed, we won't need to at all.

Our bonfire is nowhere as grand as those of my childhood Liberty Days. But as the small flickers coalesce into a certainty and then begin to blaze, we scamper back and let it burn with a curious sense of pride. Chest high we've constructed it, though much of the interior is hollow to allow the air to flow. We both know it will collapse after a while—and it does, once the blaze begins to lick past the apex—but it provides a foundation to build upon.

Like cautious fathers, all day we nurse the fire. Once it burns hot and bright, we add wetter wood to the pile so it can release its combination of steam and smoke. A column of gray haze rises high into the cloudless sky that grows thicker and darker as we increase it. Too much and the fire might not burn at all, but we find a balance. By the late afternoon, we've reached a routine in which we can relax on the plinth's far side, behind the lean-to, to avoid being kippered between feedings.

"I don't know how much of this might actually aid our situation and how much is mere busy work," admits Amodeo, as he lounges cross-legged on the rock. He gazes up at the pillar of vapor and fumes that towers high above us. "But I confess to feeling better today. Optimistic, even."

I lie in front of him with my head in his lap and allow him to toy with my hair. "It's a start," I remind him. "We've stockpiled fuel enough for two more days. If we spend some time tomorrow gathering more…"

"Without an arc blade to cut it." Rue darkens the man's words as he lifts the weapon from its resting place nearby. I hear its musical flourish as he unsuccessfully tests it once more. It's a pity that it cannot charge itself with sunlight, as does my dagger.

"We will make do." I turn onto my side and curl against him. Neither of us wears our tunics. As always upon Plum, the temperatures are warm, yet not tropical; the system's ruddy-colored sun bathes us in a golden-hour glow. "Perhaps we could start a second fire at the other corner, tomorrow?"

"Or at the next marker." Amodeo points down the Great Road, where on the opposite side, perhaps a hundred meters across and to the west, another weathered pedestal like ours abuts the avenue's edge. Unusual, to find two of these square black stones so close. Usually, they're spaced further away, like the one I can barely see to the east.

"We can manage," I assure him. "Cavemen got by without arc cutters."

"You look like a caveman." He riffles his fingers through my chest hair and winks.

"And you look like you need to be clubbed and dragged back to my cave so I can have my way with you."

"Who needs a cave?" He pulls me atop him, then thinks better of it. "No, we should put more logs on the fire."

I refuse to be pushed off. "I have a log for you, Reverend Father." I know that if—when—we rejoin the rest of the expedition, my teasing about his honorific will have to cease. Now, though, between just the two of us, that sly invocation summons a grin to his lips. "And I know just where to ignite the fire."

"Awful puns, Brother. Oh...!" The man's breathing quickens as I tug open the ties of his breeches. Two of my fingers slip between my lips. I suck them, provocation in my eyes. Then my hand dives beneath the cloth's opening and between his legs, past pole and low-hanging testicles, until I reach the whorl of flesh that is my goal. His lids narrow in reflex, pleading; he lets loose a soundless sigh.

"It's too late in the afternoon to stoke the bonfire," I whisper, urging my fingertips to massage his sweet spot. I marvel at the way his lips work as he responds to my touch. They try to summon either thanks or a plea to continue. Perhaps both. He looks into my eyes, lost in pleasure. I alone can guide him home once again. "The rains will come in another hour. We'll start again tomorrow."

His throat is dry as he rasps out, "And now?"

Softly as I can, I press my lips against his. "Now... enjoy."

He loves when I massage him in this special place. To my surprise, I've grown to love the sensations. The heat of his hole against my hand. The pliancy of that soft spot, elastic like well-kneaded dough. How moist and eager he becomes, the further I work my spit-slick fingers inside. I move the twin digits around in a circle, pressing harder and deeper. One of his legs lifts into the air and shakes, like a hound dog craving a belly rub.

I lie the man back upon the stone and pull his breeches down to the knee before I spread his legs. He reaches for the tent in my own pants, but I swat him away. This moment is solely for him. A reward for a day's good work, perhaps. A celebration of both the man and his hole. These past few days, he's ceded to me the privilege to strip away from him more than clothing. This respected, privileged leader within the Scholastic Brotherhood allows me to reduce him to the bare essentials: a man writhing upon a slab of black granite out of sheer need, craving his opening stretched. With two fingers and a load of saliva, I can transform a noted scholar into a babbling mass of nerves and muscle.

I spit on my digits once again. Work them more thoroughly inside. I relish the tension of his outer ring as I push past. When he plants his boots upon the stone and pushes upward with his hips, granting me the access I need, I praise him aloud. He becomes an accessory to his own violation, grabbing at my wrist to pull me in. But I'm in control. I unwrap his fingers and return his hand to his chest. I'm not ready to take this further. Not while I have him here, disrobed and beautiful, defenses down, trembling at every variation of my touch.

After a long day of labor, it's easy to lose track of the hour. We both revel in his pleasure. My only timekeeper is the rise and fall of Amadeo's cock as it hardens, relaxes, lolls to the side, and softens again, before stiffening whenever I push in. I add my ring finger to the other two, curling the trio slightly to cocoon inside his warm flesh, so I can watch his meat rise into the air. My free hand undoes my own ties at the waist and wraps around the erection that has been making me so uncomfortable since I started. Released from its jail, it demands reparation. I will fuck Amodeo. Oh yes. But first—

And then I feel a droplet of water upon my cheek. Tiny. A lone herald of what's soon to follow. When I startle up, I see dark clouds gathering above. I don't know whether Amodeo feels a small sprinkle himself, or whether my jolt to attention alarms him, but he sits upright, looks around, and scrambles to his feet. With an extended hand, he hauls me up. "We need to get back to camp." He snatches his arc blade and clips it to his waist before sashing up his breeches. I scramble for my recharged dagger and pull onto my shoulders what remains of my tunic.

We should have left this place half an hour ago. Part of the blame rests with the bonfire, which makes the area seem lighter than it would otherwise be. Mostly the fault is my own, for prioritizing lust over our safety. The camp is a mere five minutes away. Why hadn't I seduced him there, in the sanctuary of our circle of bramble? Neither of us needs to speak the obvious: the longer we linger here, the more chance we'll be caught in the open when the world begins its lament.

We are too late, though. It already has started.

At first, we're assaulted by vibration. No, that word is not strong enough: the landscape leaps and jolts beneath our feet. Both of us hunker down instinctively as the world seems to tilt sideways. Black stone thrums and whines. Then a storm of noise. That chilling racket of bone chafing against bone, the skull-splitting screech of hell unleashed. My hands fly to my ears. I turn to see that Amodeo has done the same. His mouth moves. He's shouting something, but I can't hear over the cacophony that seems to be all around us, on top of us. Even within us.

Wincing as he releases his head, he grabs me by the collar. Together, we jump off the stone platform. Onto the road we tumble. Over my shoulder, I watch my lean-to shiver and collapse onto the ground, then the bonfire crumble and spill. It still burns, but its thick cloud of smoke dissipates as half the embers bounce and tumble from the world's shaking. The platform's tremors shudder the buried stones of the Road, but down here, it's a fraction less intense. The tumult, though. So deafening is the dismaying sound that both Amodeo and I huddle low, palms pressed hard against our aching ears. Every nerve in my body tells me doom is imminent; every instinct commands me to run. My stomach roils. My bladder wants to loosen, though I clamp down as hard as I can to prevent soiling myself.

Forever, the commotion seems to go on. Then, just as it has every other night, it fades away, leaving the night to cower in its wake.

I rise, look up, and gasp. I see something wondrous. "Amodeo." My hands leave my still-deafened ears to tap on the man's shoulders. He faces away, still staring at the horizon, alert for danger. "Amodeo!"

"I have never been so frightened in all my years," he whispers. "Are you all right?" I have to physically turn him to face the black stone platform, to see what has appeared. His jaw drops wide. "Oh. My."

Individual particles of light now occupy the plinth. To my eyes, they resemble motes of dust caught in a head-lamp by night, only infinitely more numerous. Thousands and thousands of them swim high in the air. They do not float, like dust might—or perhaps they do, but the shape into which they have formed themselves does not change, despite their drifting. Golden the figure is, yet transparent. I can still see plainly our smoldering bonfire through the mass, which casts its own glow. Amodeo's rapt face is bathed with illumination.

"But what...?" Neither of us can quite believe what we see. Ten, fifteen meters high, the image of something alien to my sight stands before us, so incomprehensible at first that I can only take in portions of it at a time. Where it meets the stone at its base, the light forms a wide trunk that grows narrower as it ascends, covered with furrowed, bark-like skin. At its peak, a floret spreads wide, as if some titanic farmer has grown a gi-ant-sized prize broccoli and strewn its blossom with jewels. Yet I regard no vegetable: this is a living being, or at least a representation of one recreated in suspended photons. I see hollows where eyes should be; from each side project two slender wands, each sporting a number of multiply-jointed, long, slender appendages at their ends that slowly flex in more than one direction as the creature's body gently sways. "One of the Salix?" he ventures at last.

"They look like trees," I breathe. The projection even conveys personality: this being is wise. Calm. Peaceful, like the best of the Brothers themselves.

"Ayden, they do. They look like trees. See over there." Amodeo points down the great road to the next closest platform. Though its light is faded and distant, we can make out a pair of the same creatures. They lean in close together, as might Amodeo and I in an affectionate mood. "What are these...illusions?"

"Hologram memorials? Graves?" I speculate, returning my attention to the closer figure. We are but humble monkeys before this majesty. Just think of what those intricate, branch-like digits might accomplish, so many in number, compared to my ten stubs. If this is one of the Salix, what a race they must once have been. Just as my instinct had been to run, not long before, I now want to pay my respects and bow. The projection, whatever it is, is not alive, however. Even now, I can tell its movements are limited, perhaps part of a set loop. "Advertisements?"

Amodeo snorts. "If we have spent weeks in a jump ship simply to study Salice roadside billboards, I swear...waypoints along the road, perhaps? To offer cheer to travelers?" Fear forgotten, he walks around a corner to view the creation from another angle. "That racket, the one that's frightened us so, these past weeks. It seemed to arise from the stone itself. Mechanics, coming to life at nightfall? No, physical mechanics don't seem likely.

Electronics, or some sort of advanced technology. There was a sensation—maybe you felt it too—a deep, low, almost indescribable vibration…"

"Like my insides were liquifying."

"Yes. That's the one. Humans don't react very well to low-frequency vibrations. We often cannot hear them, but our bodies react. Low frequencies have been associated with so-called haunted places. They can make us feel so uncomfortable that we revert to a state of instinct and fear." He plants a hand to his chin and strolls as he theorizes, his eyes never leaving the glowing figure. "Then, the noises. Again, I don't think they arise from mechanics. Gears and such shouldn't last so long. But it's not a creature, Ayden. The noises aren't made by some boogeyman in the dark. It's these…devices!"

"The projection is going," I say, pointing up. I had been wrong to compare the creature to a broccoli. Its crown is much more complicated. But as I watch, the bejeweled, hair-like buds that cover its summit begin to disappear, though the lowermost half of the body remains. The figure flickers in and out, as a Show-Me might during a power interruption. "Going." When I turn my head to regard the twin figures down the road, they too shimmer in and out of focus. Then, without so much as a whisper, the projections of light vanish simultaneously, leaving us lit only by the remains of the bonfire at the platform's far edge. "Gone," I whisper, surprised to feel myself sad. Above, clouds collect, blotting out the stars. I feel another droplet upon my forehead.

My companion, however, is only more animated by what we'd witnessed. "But what is the source of power? How can it have survived…solar? Geothermal? No, solar is more likely. Banks of collectors. Power reservoirs. We must not have found…" He continues his walk around the platform. "These were designed to display all night, surely. But over the millennia, the forest has become overgrown…perhaps now the power sources collect only limited amounts of power. That's why the phenomenon flickers out so quickly. New conjecture: what if the sounds are not microcircuitry, but the Salice language itself? A call for repair? A summons that has gone unanswered for longer than any of our minds can fathom. Interesting."

I want to believe Amodeo's speculations. He has studied the Salix and other vanished races for more than twenty years; even his most outlandish hypotheses carry some weight. But as frightened as the expedition had been at the noises Amodeo now thinks were technological, they had not been what drove the rest of our Brothers back into orbit above the planet. No, something monstrous had been out there, somewhere in the forest, perhaps watching our every move. Something worse than the ravenous, mindless grubs had attacked the encampment. At least one person had been injured. Our team had fled an onslaught. Not noises and vibrations.

I should have spoken my mind, right then. I should have voiced what I was thinking: that we should not relax our guard, no matter our relief at discovering the uproar's source. But I do not. Nor do I stop Amodeo from his restless, excited pacing, so far from me on the platform's opposite side.

And that is why, when a massive beast I have never before seen emerges from the forest to loom above the Reverend Father, it is already too late to stop what is about to happen.

LIBERTY DAY

From nowhere, the thing materializes. I see it as an ashen shadow at first. When it advances, identical glints from the bonfire flicker across multiple obsidian eyes. White is its skin—not skin, but carapace. Not the oily white of the planet's grubs, with their unhealthy, iridescent sheen. This is the sallow white of once-buried chalk shuddered to life, or of bone assuming its ultimate and most lethal form.

I would say time slowed down in those moments when Amodeo and I balanced on opposite ends of a seesaw, he newly confident in our safety, I witnessing our doom. But it's not true. It is only I who swim in molasses while the rest of the world speeds around me. My mouth is agape, but I cannot scream; instinct roars I should scramble toward my friend and protect him, but my feet remain rooted to the ground.

As seconds pass, a few quick glimpses are all I can catch of the interloper. Whatever this thing is, it is not native to Plum. It has none of the planet's soft curves and muted colors; surely it must have been born on a place of shadow and ice. Upon two legs shaped like the hind quarters of a goat, it towers, then broadens out into a headless torso. Not featureless, like our own, but prominently sporting some sort of writhing, pulsating maw in its center. As Amodeo natters on, unawares, the creature's mouth opens like an iris, displaying a circle of teeth like stalactites. A cluster of multiple eyes gleams above the slavering mouth, as two vast, clawed arms spread with menace.

"Watch...!" My warning, commenced what feels like years ago, finally emerges from my stone lips. Amodeo pauses, cocks his head with curiosity, then follows my glance behind him. I see him startle, then attempt to clamber away from the bonfire. Something causes the creature to flinch back, but more quickly than I think possible, it dashes forward, scoops up Amodeo with no more effort than a youngling retrieving her toy doll, and scuttles off on goat legs into the forest's darkness. A massive, bony tail, its every edge a murderous razor, slashes the air as it vanishes.

I am left alone. Amodeo's cry of shock still echoes along the Road.

But Brother Witless I am not. The beast has scarcely scampered away when I leap atop the stone platform, banging my shin hard in the process. Ignoring the sharp pain, I scramble in the direction the thing has escaped. I do not think. I do not have time to think. In moments of desperation, thinking leads to indecision, indecision to failure. With Amodeo's life at stake, failure is no option.

The scent of the creature still lingers, at least until the commencing rain's petrichor overwhelms my nostrils. Like the dust of bombed-out old schoolrooms, the alien smells like decaying vellum and rotten, ancient velvet. Rainfall splashes onto my face and wets my hair as into the forest I dive, ignoring the branches that whip my face and hinder my pursuit with a hundred small fingers. At first, ahead of me, I can distinguish the crash and snap of the alien's sprint. Yet the longer and harder it rains and the farther I run, the more difficult it becomes to hear anything but the water's rataplan on the fen bladders massed overhead. Panting and desperate, I stop in a clearing and whip around, fearful that I have lost track of them.

No, Ayden. You are better than this, I reprimand, before I snivel like a child. I pull myself together. I am no scholar like Amodeo, but confronting predators in the night? Absolutely my wheelhouse. I spent my youth in the wilderness. I know how to track quarry. Finding the trail of a beast in its hasty getaway is no different.

And in many ways, easier. My confidence multiplies as I wend my way through a landscape that has grown familiar to me these last fifteen days. Plum is never entirely dark after sunset, even during its nightly storms. As my eyes adjust, I find the indicators I require. Broken branches. Moss and dead leaves trampled underfoot. Silvery bladder husks ground into dust or kicked to the side. They all are signs of passage. The edges of the thing's tail have cleaved the trunks as it strikes them. Its getaway is not subtle.

The creature has one advantage over me: it seems to know the deeper reaches of the forests quite well. Amodeo and I have followed the Great Road by day and made our nightly camps near its sides. Never have we ventured this far into the woods, where every cypress looks much the same as the next. But I follow, trying not to think—and in particular, trying not to think of the distance my enemy gains with each of my hesitations.

I am winded. My shin throbs and protests. Somewhere along the way, I've nearly twisted my ankle on an outcropping of billiard nuts. But I run on, chasing after the faintest of noises, marking the signs of footfall and hasty passage, pushing myself onward. I could easily despair and give up, but I do not. I must not.

Then the trail ends.

It shouldn't, but it does. The monster's steps lead to a small clearing and simply stop where broad cypress trunks grow close. To the left and right, no signs of breakage, no disruption. When I backtrack a few paces, I discern telltale signs of the beast's tail against cypress bark. Where the chase ends, though, nothing.

Heart pounding, I bend over, hands upon my knees, and attempt to catch my breath. So easy it would be, at this moment, to despair. Yet I will not desist. Wet hair clings to my face. Parts of me throb and ache. I have not had a proper bath in weeks, nor can I remember the last time I ate. Still, I grind my jaw and commit. For Amodeo.

That first day I'd met the Prior, he'd held out a hand from the *Beagle*'s drop dock. *Are you ready for an adventure, Sorrowful?*, he asked, staring into my eyes. And I had placed my hand in his and agreed. I didn't know what I was getting myself into. None of us had—not the expedition's taxonomist, not the others we lost in those early days. Not even Cellarer Avery. Ready or not, the excitement we sought found us first.

When one accepts an invitation to adventure, one waives the right to choose in what form adventure arrives.

Then I hear it. A noise, not very far away. I hold my breath, will my heightened pulse to still itself. I hear it again. An anomaly—something not of the planet called Plum, but from my own. A tinny, electronic scale that travels up an octave, then immediately back down again. Amodeo's depleted arc blade. He must be attempting to revive it for his own self-defense.

Once again, the blade powers on and instantly off. This time, it almost bleats annoyance. So close, it seems. I could almost reach out and...then I discover what I had missed before. I'd assumed the close-growing trees where the trail ended were trunks, but they are merely the more pliant upper reaches of a mature cypress. I can easily push them aside and shove through.

Upon doing so, however, I find myself sliding and tumbling down a steep slope, head over ass, until I land shoulders-first upon something hard and unyielding. Dozens of bladders pushed downward by the rainfall tangle my limbs as I descend, battering me like toy balloons and failing to cushion my fall. Whatever it is reacts with surprise, bucking me off so that I tumble some more. I see something chalky and grim scrambling away from the spot where we had collided. My enemy. And stooped beyond it, Amodeo.

Blood streams from a gash on his forehead. His curls are matted with the stuff. I don't like the limp, dead look of his left arm, dangling useless by his side. He crouches on alert, however, non-functioning arc blade in his functioning hand. There's even less light in this ditch than upon the forest floor, a full three meters above. "I think you upset it," he pants.

"I upset *it?!*"

The beast opens its circular maw, exposing its teeth. Its tail whips around as it gauges us both. Having no head to turn, it backs away at an oblique angle to keep us both in view, seemingly wary. My hand grasps for my slingshot, which is still tucked into the waistband of my breeches.

"Don't panic it." Amodeo's voice is weakening. I know he can't hold out that much longer. Not with so much blood staining his face and chest.

The trench in which we stand is a nest, I realize. A bedlike platform of salvaged stone and soft leaves occupies a dry corner. Around it sits in a pile a number of ebony, glossy, shoebox-sized blocks, strung together upon a single thick black cable. Each flat surface glows with dark red rune-like symbols. Technology of some sort. Obviously important.

The creature has chosen a well-defended camp, I begrudgingly admit. Invisible, among its walls of mature cypress trunks. Darker and more forbidding than the forest proper. As I'd discovered on my fall, the fen bladders here cluster thickly at the level of the ground above, their tendrils just out of reach, like hundreds of paper streamers at an old-fashioned prom. If it weren't for the diffuse red light of the alien's salvage, we wouldn't be able to see much of anything at all.

"I'll make it a deal," I call out. "I'll try not to panic the damned thing, and it agrees to stop kidnapping you. Sound fair?"

The creature's mouth widens and gyrates in a way that makes my stomach twist. That mouth is hunger itself. I intend to be nowhere near when it begins to consume. "Ayden..." Amodeo weakly cautions.

I know I sound angry. I am angry. I'm furious. "Let him go," I snap at the thing that stands between us. "*Let him go!*" The alien's tail lashes out sinuously, whipping from side to side like an angry feline. I temper the steel in my voice and try another approach. "You can't understand me. But you know what I'm here for." I point to the Prior. "Let me take him away. We'll both leave you alone. Look at him. He's not well."

The creature shifts its eyes in Amodeo's direction. Then, as if answering my plea with contempt, its tail thrashes out with force to smite my companion squarely on the side of the head.

This time, Amodeo falls to his knees, a deadness in his eyes. "Ayden. Love." His arc blade falls from his slackened grasp shortly before he topples unconscious onto it.

"No!"

But the thing isn't finished. With unerring precision, the tail whips my way and retracts, poised with both the grace and menace of a swan's neck. Then it strikes again, this time snaking around my side and stabbing so quickly that I have no time to avoid its attack. Pain radiates from my right buttock. My hand flies to my behind and comes away wet.

The agony is beyond anything I've experienced. Worse than the toothache I had when I was ten or the nightmare extraction that followed, performed by one of the uncles brandishing a pair of pliers and a bottle of ether. Worse than the time one of my brothers shoved me through the hatch of a bunker and I hit the ground three meters below, breaking my arm in two places. Far worse than my throbbing shin. I want to die. I want to fall to my knees and topple over, as Amodeo had, so I could writhe and grimace and shout obscenities at the top of my voice.

Instead, I grit my teeth and fight through. "Motherfucker!" I roar, resurrecting the impolite language of my youth. I'd nearly lost my grip on the slingshot when the thing attacked me, but I hold it at the ready in my right hand while my left fishes a billiard nut tucked into the ties of my breeches. With all the expertise of someone who grew up hunting squirrels in the Carolinas, I load the sphere into the weapon's makeshift cradle, haul back on the elastic, and let it fly.

My projectile lands with an audible hard clack on one of its black eyes, ricocheting upward to stir the undersides of the bladders. "Ha!" I immediately regret my exultant crow when another spasm from my ass causes me almost to double over. The creature is so taken aback by my assault that it retreats several meters to the ravine's side. "That's right." Growling, I rummage for another nut. I haul back, squint, and let it fly. Once again, it connects with the alien, striking it squarely in the center of its cluster of eyes with the sound of a hammer striking a nail.

Its mouth opens in anger, all the more unsettling for its menacing asymmetry. It lets out a shrill squeal, perhaps of pain, perhaps calling for aid. I feel a savage pang of satisfaction to know the creature suffers at my hand. More important, though, is that the being leaves a clear path to scurry to Amodeo's side. The Prior still lives; his breathing seems shallow, though, and I am not heartened by his pallor.

The creature does not like me rejoining my companion. It advances, hissing like a tomcat, tail whipping from side to side. I whip out another billiard nut and pull back as hard as I can in the moment's heat, knocking it so hard on its goat leg that it stumbles and reels. "You want more?" My voice is as deafening as I've ever heard it, but never have I been pushed to such an extreme. "I'll give you more! Oh, I'll give you a lot more."

In a cruel twist of irony, there is no more. Cursing, I pat my sore abdomen, searching for ammunition, but I have exhausted my supply of nuts. All three have bounced out of reach, and I cannot politely pardon myself to the thing and collect them for another go.

Sensing that I have depleted my resources, the alien rallies. Mouth wide, razor-point teeth bared, it takes a step toward the two of us. Then another.

I drop to my knees. Amodeo's blade lies within an arm's reach, but without power, it's as useful as a cello bow. My arc dagger is my last line of defense, so I withdraw it from its scabbard and finger the safety. A ten-centimeter energy blade versus an arsenal of deadly teeth and a meter-and-a-half-long spiked tail—that's a fair fight, right?

Well. If this is how it ends, so be it. Tears spring to my eyes as I consider how much more time I'd wanted with

Amodeo. Fourteen days alone together, four days of intimacy. That's all we'd shared in the end. Yet after so many years of running and hiding, of cell time, of training for something better, this meager handful of days has shown me how and with whom I should spend the rest of my life.

I'm down to the last few grains in that hourglass. Yet I want more. I want so much more. If all I have left to keep that beast away from Amodeo's unconscious figure is one stubby little cutter—fine. One stubby little cutter will have to do. Safety off, I rotate the lever with my middle finger to the highest weapon setting. "Come at me then." Though every inch of me throbs with pain, though I'm soaked with rain and sweat and blood, I stare down the beast, daring it. "But I won't be an easy fight."

I stagger to my feet and feel the dagger thrum in my grip as I power it up. The bright current lights up the immediate area like a lantern. The alien had been advancing when I spoke, preparing its onslaught. Yet at the dagger's sudden radiance, barnacled lids snap shut over those lustrous multiple eyes. The being leaps back, seemingly in surprise. Maybe even fear.

I'm taken aback at the reaction, but I immediately capitalize upon it. "You don't like that? No?" I make stabbing motions in the alien's direction, noticing how it angles its body away from the cutter's dazzle and shuts its maw tight. Various lids peek open, then snap closed. Its tail lashes sideways, furious. "What? You don't like light?"

I'm onto something. Puzzle pieces click into place. How it flinches from the arc's blaze. This dark enclosure below ground, away from even the night sky's purple hue. How the creature had staggered by the road when Amodeo exposed it to the bonfire's gleam, scattered and diminished as it was by that point. Even the glowing symbols upon its technology are a dull red, as if fashioned for light-averse eyes. The creature is photophobic. Like an underground or deep-sea organism, it is sensitive to anything bright.

Armed with this realization, I snap the cutter's setting to burn. As a weapon, the arc dagger can eventually saw through anything short of stone, but though this utility setting is less dangerous, it flares much brighter. The arc dances and vibrates a brilliant white that causes the being to hasten away from me. "That's right." My voice rings out above the lessening rain. I continue to bellow. "I figured it out, you son of a bitch. Get out. Get away from here."

But the creature doesn't go.

I might have gained an advantage, but I realize with dismay that it's temporary. Overwhelmed though those eyes may be for the moment, they'll adjust soon enough. I'm not wielding a stage spotlight, after all. Already, I can see the unblinking cluster beginning to unseal again, each lid wider and wider as it looks past the dagger to the pair of us. I totter forward, limping, brandishing my poor weapon. "Get out!" Over and over, I repeat the words as if they might be the ward that protects me. "Get *out!*"

All the alien's lids are now open. Blinking. Judging me. I know it's calculating an attack. But guess what, you misbegotten piece of shit? I'm calculating mine, too. My eyes dart around the enclosure, desperate for anything else I might weaponize.

What I really need is a bigger light. Something dazzling. That slow-release waterproof explosive would sure come in handy, just about now. But there's nothing I can use. Nothing.

Until I look above me, at the fen bladders. Slowly their bodies rise, now that the rain has slackened and no longer beats them groundward. I've never seen them in such a dense cluster before, but the way tree trunks have grown around this gulch has corralled them close by the hundreds. Maybe thousands.

Oh, I realize. Thousands of floating sacs of flammable hydrogen.

The alien pulls itself to its full height upon those unearthly goat legs and spreads wide its clawed arms. Its eyes are fully open. Tail poised to strike.

Only one course of action remains. I raise my arm high above my head, arc dagger still set to burn. I touch it to the nearest dangling, wispy tendrils, so much like dried Spanish moss, before they can rise completely out of reach.

The creature and I both watch as a spark kindles. The flame licks up the filaments toward the fen bladder's body, gathering speed and size as it burns. All at once, a single bladder's skin bursts with a pop; the hydrogen that had kept it aloft ignites in a gout of brilliant flame.

Those flames leap to other tendrils. Detonation by detonation, fire and light spread outward in a circle.

I drop my arm and cock my head at the fucking monster aghast before me, certain of my victory.

The holocaust that follows unfolds more quickly than I can reckon, tipping from blaze to conflagration to inferno in mere seconds. The yellow sun of home never seemed as bright as the supernova happening right over my head; heat the weight of an anvil pushes me to my knees as bladder after fen bladder erupts with exponential speed and intensity. What rain that still falls cannot stop the chain reaction. The circle of hell widens so quickly that all the oxygen around me dissipates to feed the angry flames.

Gasping for breath and with a spinning head, I throw myself atop Amodeo and cradle his head to safeguard him from the falling ash and debris. This maelstrom is all my doing. I have summoned upon the planet Plum a light brighter than it has seen in many a long epoch. I am Sorrowful no longer, but Prometheus of legend, bringer of fire.

Brother Prometheus. How I very much like the sound of my new name.

The creature's screech chills me to the bone. When I dare look up, its obsidian eyes have calcified, grown milky and brittle. Blinded. Around the ditch it thrashes, still shrieking as if mortally wounded. Finding the incline I'd fallen down earlier, it scrabbles its way back to the forest floor. Beneath a sky that still rains the ash and fire of countless fen bladders, the alien runs off on all fours with a lament of dismay. I hear it collide unseeing into cypress trunks as it flees.

Cinders smolder in my hair and upon the rags that used to be my tunic. I roll off Amodeo and beat them out. My backside throbs in agony, but it's a flesh wound. No nerves or tendons damaged. My companion still breathes, though his arm lies at an ungainly angle.

I know how to bandage wounds and set a bone that has broken. I will carry out those duties for him once I gather my strength. Somehow, I will transport Amodeo to the Great Road. The alien's strange boxes I will claim as well—they are too valuable an artifact to be left behind. I will give Amodeo full credit for discovering them.

For a moment, though, just for one quiet, weary moment for myself, I roll upon my back and regard the stars. The cypresses are too waterlogged to have been affected by the swift conflagration; I spy singe marks upon some, but no real damage. A few fen bladders still float above, somehow escaped from my ecological carnage.

But for once, I can stare up at Plum's violet sky with my view unimpeded, Amodeo's still hand beneath my own.

Then, as I listen, at a distance I hear the unexpected uproar of the Great Road's mechanisms coming to life. Had the blaze I'd set somehow refueled their energy reservoirs? There would have been light enough, if that's what fed them. What once had been jarring, un-earthly timbres sound less frightening to my ears; now I know the gentle beings they had served.

I may not see them from down here in this trench, cov-ered with the grit and soot of cremated flora, but I close my eyes and imagine those golden figures upon their platforms, delineating the route. I wonder if the Salix ever considered the possibility that one day, far in their futures, their incarnations of air and photons would linger still to greet other races traversing their strange and unfamiliar highway.

Yet every road has a source. A destination. Byways in between. Any species with a claim to wisdom knows a road is nothing without its travelers. How fortunate I have been to tread Plum's great granite thoroughfare with Amodeo as my companion.

I open my eyes again. High above, one star burns brighter than the others. By the moment, it grows more incandescent. Then, as I watch, all around the star blos-soms a shining, brilliant sphere. As luminance flares into flame, the object begins leaving in its wake a track of hot gas and ions. I am witnessing a spacecraft's plasma trail as it enters the atmosphere.

Our expedition's shuttle. The *Beagle* has finally located us, summoned by my massive firestorm with the two of us at its center.

"Amodeo," I whisper, squeezing his hand. He cannot reply. "My brother. We are not abandoned." The Prior had promised that a sign would be delivered to our watchful crew. Neither of us knew I would be its messenger. "Don't worry. They won't be long, now."

I pull myself to my knees and drape my companion's arm around my shoulder. This last leg of our journey may be the most trying. When the Brothers aboard the shuttle discover Amodeo and me—and they will—I do not intend for them to fish us out of this squalid pit. No. They will find us beside the Great Road, perhaps a little worse for wear, waiting among the luminous, serene figures of the Salix.

There, Amodeo and I shall meet them arm in arm. Hand in hand. Exactly as we mean to continue.

ACKNOWLEDGMENTS

I'm grateful to Peter Schutes, whose question, "Could you possibly write a story about a road in outer space?" afforded me an opportunity to revisit the universe of the United Settlements I'd created in my other science fiction novella, *Journey's End*. From such an unlikely prompt arose a writing experience that was purely pleasurable—and as someone who's made a career out of putting ideas to paper, I can attest that's a rare thing indeed.

I must also thank my friends Al and Guar for reviewing this story in a late draft stage, and for allowing me to pepper them afterward with way too many questions. Both gentlemen offered insights that realigned my perspective upon what I'd written. For that, I'm indebted.

ABOUT THE AUTHORS

Frank Slater pops in from time to time. He is a historian of mid-twenty-first century science fiction and has been involved in the creation of the retrospective oral history of speculative arts project, *Hindsight*. When not moving through the temporal sphere, he has occasionally partaken in writing science fiction. His stories and essays appear in many literary tomes, such as the Peter Schutes pulp paperback, "Same Sex", *Simultaneous Times,* and various critical journals.

J. W. Steed is a pseudonym for the author of more than a dozen mainstream novels. He also writes memoir and humorous essays. He teaches creative writing in the metro NYC area and is active in the Science Fiction and Fantasy Writer's Association (SFWA). Steed's writings appear in the bestsellers *Dirty Dorms and Fresh Men, Come Young and Old*, and *Same Sex*. He has a cult following who can't wait to read more! You can read Mr. Steed's blog at mrsteed64.blogspot.com

ALSO FROM PETER SCHUTES PUBLISHING

Please visit Peter's Website to find links to all of Peter's books.

PAPERBACKS

The Autobiography of Peter Schutes

Big Bodies of All Sizes

Big Hole River

Bobbing Buoys and Salty Seamen

Confessions of a Rodeo Clown

Cosmic Cage: Gay SF Erotica

Dirty Dorms and Fresh Men

Filthy Jobs and Steamy Showers

The Gospel of Priapus

Hoboes, Hustlers, and Outlaws

Hot Blue Collars

Like the Greeks Do

Mowing and Blowing

Muscle Bottom

Same Sex: Gay SF Clone Erotica

Satanic Seductions

The Slaves of Rome

Small Cockpits and Big Hangars

Tales of Two Daddies

E-BOOKS

The Able Seaman

The Anaconda Copper

The Artist

The Autobiography of Peter Schutes
Backwoods Delivery
Billy Club
Buck Private
Bunkhouse Buddies
The Butt Baby
Chopper Jock
Cloistered
Coached
Dark as a Dungeon
Demonic Deception *aka* Deceived, Cursed & Blessed
Desert Island Daddies
Dutch Treat
Edging the Lawn
The Expectant Member
Firehouse Lovers
The Fish
Five Erotic Tales
Hercules and Lippos
Hobo Honey
Hotshot
Little Shamus
Logger's Delight
On the Block
Panama Heat
Satan's Sissy Boy
The Spotter
Steroid Steve
The Thigh Baby
Under the Boardwalk

Wee Dobbin

World's Biggest

***** Coming Soon *****

PAPERBACKS

Tales of Two More Daddies

E-BOOKS

The Artist

Billy Club

The City Gardener

Edging the Lawn

The Good Dad

In Each Other's Arms

Lift Pump

The Longshoremen

The Most Dangerous Flower

The Orchardman

Poolside Plantings

Slapjack

Tuxes n' Tails